So You  with a little magic.

Miranda A. Reid

MW00880669

DEDICATION

Special thanks to all of my family and friends who encouraged me to keep writing.

Thank you to graphic designer Dionna Gary and ThreeLittlebeesphotography.

Dedicated to my aunt, Darlene Palermo. I love you and will always miss you.

With A Little Magic.

Copyright © 2017 Miranda Reid
All rights reserved.
ISBN: **1984194151**

Chapter 1

The beginning of my fear: public school

Knock Knock,

Mya's diary thoughts out loud: That was the sound that terrified me. The sound of my mom knocking on my door to wake me up for school. Today is the day that I feared, the day I never wanted to come, the day of doom. My very first day going to public school, starting the eighth grade. My name is Mya Iverson, and I am a thirteen-year-old girl with dreadlocks who was diagnosed with cerebral palsy at birth. Cerebral Palsy may sound like something you've never heard before. But it is the disease that has made me weird. It has caused me to be different from every other kid around me. The kids in my neighborhood won't dare play with me, invite me over or even say hello.

Mom asked me if I would like to ride the bus to school today. Is she crazy? There was no way in this world that I would be riding the yellow bus to school. There are so many thoughts running through my brain, that my brain is probably going to explode any minute now. First things first, how do kids dress for public school? I'm guessing jeans and sneakers will do. That's what I'll be wearing.

"Are you ready? ," Mom asked.

My thoughts were screaming "no," but I replied, "yes mom."

"You are going to be just fine, remember that God made you different for a reason, a very good reason. One day you'll find out what that reason is." Said, mom.

Mom smiles at me with a lot of confidence showing on her face.

My mom has always tried her best to make me feel very special. She is the one who allowed me to get my dreadlocks done. My dad is awesome, but he did not want me to get them. He was totally against it. He felt as though I was too young. I felt like getting dreadlocks would be an adventure to me and it was.

Mom looks very nervous as we are pulling up to the school. She is trying her very best to keep a smile on her face for me, but I know that she is extremely worried. It is now my job to make her feel better.

"Okay mom we are here, please don't worry. I'm a big girl, and I'm ready for this!" I assured her.

"Have your teacher or nurse call me if you need anything, I'm very proud of you. Have a good day. Remember being different is a positive thing. Love you," said mom.

I replied, "Love you too". And got out of the car.

My condition has gotten better over the years and that is why my doctor said It would be okay for me to finally attend public school, even without an aid with me every minute of the day. I have a wheelchair and a walker because sometimes my joints tighten up and it gets hard to walk. Sometimes my speech is not very clear, and my walking is far from normal. But I am happy that I've made progress. There was a time when I could not walk at all. I'm glad those days are long gone!

Ring ring ring! I jumped in fear from the sound of the loud bell that rang.

Another sound that frightens me. I'm guessing that was the bell for class.

There are kids running through the hallway, almost knocked me down! Boys and girls holding hands, kids playing in the bathrooms, and teachers trying to get everyone to class. This is a nightmare. I just need to find room A45.

My heart began to rapidly beat, and my palms began to sweat.

"Excuse me, sir, can you show me where room A45 is?" I asked.

"Of course, I will, my name is Mr. Davids and I am a guidance counselor here at Springville Middle school." He replied.

"Thank you, my name is Mya Iverson and nice to meet you," I said back to who I now know as Mr. Davids. He is the first person to speak to me and it was pleasant.

"Here you are Ms. Mya Iverson, A45." Said Mr. Davids as he walked away.

I took a deep breath before entering the classroom and remember my mother's words.

I walk into the classroom, luckily everyone has not made it to class yet. I thought for sure I'd be walking into a full classroom of kids staring at me and my funny walk and sometimes odd appearance. But I lucked out. They're coming in one by one…as my heart drops. At least I beat them to the classroom.

The eyes are starting to look at me, the whispers begin. But I will ignore. Well try at least. I'm already starting to question if this was a good idea. Should I have even tried to be normal, or fit in with regular kids? I'm not normal or regular. But I'm here now.

"Are you in the right class?" asked a girl with long blonde hair and freckles as she chuckles.

"Is this United States history?" I replied to the rude girl.

She ignored me.

Some people may be wondering why I was placed in a regular class and not a special needs class. My doctor approved it, and my at-home teacher said I would be just fine. Cerebral Palsy affects me physically more than anything, which is unusual. But I am unusual. Which is why when this class ends, I'll sit and wait for everyone else to leave to avoid being pushed passed or laughed at. My walk is my biggest challenge. My mom and dad feel that I will walk normal one day.

I shrugged, and finally got up to leave.

This is going to be the longest day of my life. This day began at 8:30 am and my mom will be waiting for me at 3:00 pm.

I was constantly checking the clock, anxiously waiting to go home.

I have six class periods to attend each day, and I have to check in with the school nurse after lunch.

"Mya Iverson, you are wanted in the main office," said my history teacher.

I remember where the main office is because it was the first door when I walked into the building, so I didn't dare ask her. I was already embarrassed enough. Feeling and being embarrassed will probably be a norm for me. Staying home may not have been a bad idea. What can possibly come out of this? Now, I'm wondering why I would be needed in the main office? I just got here. Literally just got here!

I walked to the main office using my walker to see who was calling.

"Are you Mya Iverson?" asked a lady at the desk.

I replied, "Yes, I am."

"Your mother is on the phone for you." Says the lady.

Great. My mom is going to start stalking me while I'm only away for a few hours at school. Well, I guess we're both on edge for now. It is only the first day.

"Hi mom," I said.

"Honey I am just so worried about you, how is your day going so far? Are you in any pain?" asked mom.

"I'm fine mom," I replied.

"Okay, I'll be there at 3:00 on the dot to pick you up!" Mom said.

"Bye mom, I'll see you later," I replied, and then hung up.

I walked back to the class using my walker, dropping my head in embarrassment.

Ring ring ring! The bell rings again.

I looked through my schedule to find my next class as students ran through the hall passing me by. I was wishing someone would offer to help me find all of my classes, but no one has even stopped for a second.

Later in the day after several classes, I noticed a boy staring at me. I get extremely nervous wondering what in the world is he looking at.

"Hello, do you need help finding your class?" says a boy with curly red hair and overalls.

I wanted to ignore him so badly, but something told me to speak because this may be my one and only chance at a friendship.

So, I replied, "Sure, I'm heading to the cafeteria and I am not exactly sure of what direction to head in. This school is pretty big."

"Hmmm, if I show you where the cafeteria is what do I get back in return?" asked the mysterious red-headed boy wearing overalls.

So now, I am extremely confused at this moment. I have no idea what he even means. What am I supposed to offer besides a thank you? Is he simply joking around, or is he being serious? Man, I really need more experience with this social stuff. I better respond quickly, before he realizes how much of a weirdo I truly am.

"I take it that you are joking, right?" I asked.

"Joking? No, I was being very serious. You can repay me by simply sitting with me at the lunch table. I usually sit alone." He replied.

"You got it!" I said.

I and this mysterious boy who hasn't shared his name yet are walking towards the cafeteria. Eyes are on us as we enter the cafeteria.

"Let's sit here," says the boy.

"May I ask your name?" I asked.

"I was wondering when you would ask, you first!" says the boy.

"My name is Mya Iverson, now what is yours?" I asked him again.

"I like that, It's like the basketball player. You know Allen Iverson" says the boy.

"Don't remind me." I said while rolling my eyes.

"Well my name isn't as cool as yours, but my name is Steven Roberts." Says the mysterious curly red headed boy who has just revealed his name to me.

Now I am wondering what comes next. Is this boy my friend or is he being nice to me out of pity? Anyone who sees me automatically assumes that I am in need of help because my disease is very visible to the natural eye. So, I've had many people pity me, but no actual friends. I thought that school would be the place to change that. I guess thinking the worst won't help either though. I just wish people knew that my brain functions well. I may walk and talk funny sometimes, but my brain is fine.

"That's a nice name, at least you don't have people asking you if you're related to Allen Iverson all the time, or my favorite is when they ask me for free basketball game tickets," I said while giggling with Steven.

"Well if I were you I'd play along and tell them yes ha-ha!" says Steven as he stares at me making me feel a little uncomfortable.

Why does he keep staring at me, maybe I'm starting to talk funny and he's noticing? Socializing just may be overrated.

"So, do you have any friends around here?" I asked out of pure curiosity.

"Ehh I wouldn't call them friends. I would say two friends that I speak with every now and then, but we all keep to ourselves around here. I'll introduce you to them though." Steven replied.

"Where have you been, did you just move into town or something?" asked Steven.

Okay now, this is where I get a little freaked out. Why is he asking me this or am I over thinking things? Do I be honest or just make something up? I guess being honest may be my best bet if I'm looking to have friends. Going to public school will be much easier with at least one good friend. So here goes nothing.

"Well, it's kind of a long story, but I'll try to cut it short. My parents chose to have me homeschooled up until now. I was diagnosed with a disorder called cerebral palsy at birth and my parents felt being home was best. They believed having a teacher and nurse come to our house every day would be more beneficial than sending me to school. My mother and father also feared that I'd be teased for my speech and the way I walk. I've gotten a lot better now, but when I was younger my condition was stronger. Myself, parents and my doctor felt that it was okay for me to begin attending public school with other kids now. So here I am today. My very first day of attending a public school like a regular kid." I said very quickly.

"Well, I'm glad that you are here. Maybe now I'll have a real friend finally. I think It took true courage for you to come here. I'm not sure that I would've had the same courage. You're my shero." Says Steven.

"What's a shero?" I embarrassingly asked.

"A shero is a hero that is a woman silly, and that's what you are to me. You kicked Cerebral Palsy's butt!" yelled Steven.

"Well, thank you. Nobody ever said anything like that to me before and I'm pretty new to this whole socializing thing. The only people I get to talk to are adults and my little German shepherd named King. He's so adorable. My dad gave him to me as a gift." I said.

"I'd like to meet him one day. Maybe if I ever get an invitation to hang out after school sometime. Hint Hint!" Says Steven., trying to get an invitation to my house.

"Well, what's your deal? Why are you so nice? Why don't you have many friends? I shared with you my life story, tell me something." I said.

"Well, way to get straight to the point Ms. Iverson." Says Steven.

Steven and I laugh and giggle together.

"Well are you going to answer?" I asked.

"Yes. But my answer will be confusing because I am a confusing guy. I guess that's why I don't have many friends. I've never really been able to fit in with anyone, sometimes I wonder if something is wrong with me but eventually I stopped wondering. I don't have the best home life. My parents are together, but our home is not happy. I choose to keep to myself usually. I'm usually too focused on my home life to even make friends, but at this point, I really need to start making friends and doing things that kids do. I hope that was a good enough answer for you because right now that's all I've got." said Steven.

Steven and I just sat for a moment and stare at each other. I can't help but wonder about his home life more.

"Well I've never fit in either so that makes two of us. You've got a friend in me, Mr. Roberts." I assured him.

Steven and I exchanged phone numbers, smile and go on to our separate classes.

I've been going from class to class and so far, only three people have spoken to me, the guidance counselor, the jerk in class who asked if I was in the right place, and now my new friend Steven Roberts. Well, this is not great but I must admit, I'm happy to have met someone nice. I don't feel as alone anymore. I wish we had more class periods together though.

So, I go to my last class of the day which is mathematics, and the classroom was full by the time I got there. It took me a little longer to walk to this class because of the distance from where I began walking. I sit down in the only chair available, in the very front row. The teacher hands us classroom guidelines and expectations. She begins to read over them and says that's all we will be doing today. Well great, this shouldn't take long. I guess I'll just be sitting here until the bell rings. I can literally feel the eyes burning into the back of my head. The discomfort begins. I hear the whispers.

"Class, please refer to the number one guideline which is respect. When I am speaking refrain from having side conversations!" Says the mathematics teacher.

So, it wasn't just me that heard the whispers and side conversations. I need to just stop paying attention to other kids and focus on making it through my first day. The teacher stops reading over the classroom guidelines and expectations and says that for the rest of the period we can talk to each other until the bell rings, as long as we keep the volume down. Well, she doesn't have to worry about my volume. As I'll be sitting here in complete and total silence. Everyone runs to their friends, and I'm just sitting here. I guess these friend groups were formed years ago in first grade while I was home learning to speak properly.

"Ms. Iverson, or can I call you Mya?" Asked the teacher.

"Mya is fine," I replied.

"You don't need to sit alone, maybe try mingling with other students. Try making friends." Said the teacher.

I literally just sat and stared at her until finally, I spoke back.

"Maybe another time Ms." I firmly said.

"Ms. Kelly is my name, and okay I won't force you but the school will be pretty lonely without making friends. Your experience will be much more pleasant having someone to talk to." She said.

Ms. Kelly walks away and goes back to her desk. She started to watch me closely for the rest of class.

I appreciate her care, but there was no way in the world I was going to make a fool out of myself by trying to fit in with those kids. Well, the last period of the day, and even teachers have not really welcomed me or made me feel like this was a safe place.

But maybe it's better this way. I don't want any special attention or any special treatment. I wanted to be regular and that's what I seem to be getting. Adjusting will be difficult, but at least I faced my biggest fear of even stepping foot in this school. And hey, I did make a friend today. Steven Roberts. Tomorrow will be another challenge though. It's a different world here, and this is only the beginning.

Chapter 2

Facing my fears again: Or faking it until I make it.

The first day of my biggest fear is over and I am still alive. Maybe I'm a little over the top, but my fear of attending public school was strong. It gave me nightmares. I'm not quite sure if it's going to get harder or easier but only time will tell. I will tell my parents about Steven, the guidance counselor, and teacher. I'll be sure to leave out the stares, rude question, and giggles. Mom and dad get worried so easily when it comes to me. I guess you can say that I am pretty fortunate to have caring parents. Well here they come, ready to hear all about my first day of class.

"So, tell us all about your day, how was school?" Mom asked anxiously as dad waits to hear my response.

"My day was actually better than expected!" I said with a half-smile.

"Really that's great! I'm so glad to hear that. Did anything special happen during the day?" Asked mom.

"Baby, we want to hear about everything." Said, dad.

"Well, nothing too special. The first person to speak to me was a guidance counselor named, Mr. Davids. He showed me to my class when I was really lost. I also met a nice boy named Steven Roberts. He's nice. Oh, and one particular teacher that had actually taken the time out to speak to me and suggested that I try making friends." I answered back to my parents.

"Let's back up to this Steven character, I want more details about him!" Dad said as mom rolled her eyes.

"Honey you can tell us more at another time, I know you are probably exhausted from such a long day. You should head upstairs and relax." Mom said.

Dad grunts and crosses his arms and legs as he is still very interested in who Steven was.

I hope that my parents aren't thinking that I have a crush on Steven just because he's a boy. He's just a friend that happens to be a boy. Having a crush is the last thing on my mind. I'm trying to survive the eighth grade. I am going to shower then lay in bed planning my tomorrow.

I showered, changed clothes and then went to bed to relax. The entire time I was seriously stressing out, and my mind wouldn't stop racing.

I'm starting to think, and all of my clothes are old. I need new clothes that will make me fit in a little better. I wonder if mom and dad will take me shopping for different clothes. I don't think my baggy pants and old sneakers will do. I've never been into fashion or clothing styles, but I'm thinking maybe it is time for new changes. I mean, that's what this school thing is all about for me, change.

"Mom!!" I yelled.

"WHAT, WHAT," my mom responds frantically thinking that something awful has happened.

"Sorry, I didn't mean to scare you. But I was really wondering if you and dad could take me shopping for a few things. I would like to wear some new styles of clothing to school. My old stuff is not cutting it for school mom" I asked.

"Well, this is interesting. I'm sure your dad would be okay with it. We'll take you to the mall over the weekend to get somethings, honey." Said, mom.

"Thank you, mom. I just want a change." I said.

I have no idea what clothes to buy, but I know they have to be better than the clothing already hanging in my closet. I didn't really go anywhere prior to now, so I basically wore sweatpants and tee-shirts every day. Definitely, do not want to dress like that in school.

All I can do is sit and think about things I can do to fit in more at school. It's bad enough I stand out so much because of my disability. Speaking of, I probably should be working hard at home to walk better. My walk just screams, "crippled." I hate this so much. The fact that I am sitting in bed trying to find ways to fix myself to fit in. For now, I'll just try to get a good night's rest for my second day of school tomorrow.

I went to sleep with a lot on my mind, full of mixed emotions and scary thoughts about school.

The next day.

Well, I'm on my way back to Springville middle school, for another day of constant butterflies and nerves running through my stomach. It feels like there is a party going on in my stomach. My nerves need to calm down.

Day two of public school with a bunch of strangers. Here goes nothing…

I saw Steven across the hall coming towards me really fast. I'm surprised to see him so early. It is almost as if he was waiting for me.

"Hey Mya wait up for me!" yelled Steven.

I waved and smiled back at Steven.

"I wish we had class periods together, instead of just having lunch," Steven said.

"Imagine how I feel." I replied.

"It must be pretty difficult not knowing anyone, but then again I've been around these people for years and still nobody hardly ever speaks to me. Only when they're telling me to move or get out of the way. Or my favorite, when they ask me to help with their homework. I guess all lonely kids are nerds who get straight A's ha-ha." Steven said while laughing.

"That makes me feel like there is no hope for making friends at all. Thanks" I said sarcastically.

"Hey, just being honest" Steven replied.

"I'm sure. But I'm not too sure I want to be surrounded by so many people, yet still feel alone. In that case, I could be home in bed or playing with my dog." I said.

Steven and I shook our heads and look around at all the other kids that are standing by themselves.

Ring Ring Ring! The bell rings for the first period to start.

"Oh shoot, I'm going to be late," I said. "Time fly's when you're having fun," Steven says jokingly.

"See ya at lunch." Steven yells as he runs down the hall to his class.

I made it to class, and surprisingly I'm not nervous anymore. Maybe Steven has something to do with that. Who knows. I've got a seat in the back and of course, the stares were there. The whispering was there again too. I guess my walker is amusing to some people. This is so weird for me because everyone at home is use to my disabilities and special needs. I feel normal at home, and here I feel like an outcast. Already.

There is a girl in this class with long black hair and big glasses that was not here yesterday. I wonder why she missed the first day of school. I kind of want to sit next to her. She doesn't seem to be a part of any cliques so far. I came to school to learn, but also with high hopes of making some friends. Everyone in the class is talking and gossiping because the teacher hasn't entered the classroom yet. There is an empty seat by her, maybe I'll sit there. It's worth a shot. Why not. Be brave Mya, I said to myself.

I got up to introduce myself to the unknown girl with black hair and big glasses. I hope that this unknown girl will be in need of a friend.

"Hi, my name is Mya Iverson," I said in a very nervous voice tone.

"Hi, I'm Corrine" The unknown girl who we now know as Corrine replied.

"I'm new here at this school, I was homeschooled. Thought I'd say hello. I don't remember seeing you in this class yesterday." I said.

"Oh well welcome to…school. School is school. And oh yeah, I couldn't be here yesterday. Thanks for coming over." Corrine replied as she turned her head.

I am a little disappointed in the dry response from Corrine. I just assumed that Corrine would be a little friendlier. I guess not.

"Welcome back class. Today is the second day of class which means the actual book work begins. Excuse my tardiness, I had an important phone call to take in the main office regarding my son." Says the teacher of my first period class.

The teacher hands out books and tells students to take their pencils out so that they can begin taking notes as she teaches the first lesson.

United States history was the one class that I was looking forward to because my grandmother was a history teacher, and now it just feels awkward. My grandmother was a history teacher, and she would teach me at home all the time. My grandmother made it interesting and taught things ahead of my grade level. She even taught me things that most schools don't teach. History is definitely my all-time favorite subject, but this class is not going to be my favorite at all. I can already tell. The vibe is even horrible in here.

I sat in class feeling a little down. I felt that my attempt to make a friend was a failure and that nobody in that class would speak to me. The teacher goes onto her lesson, and I just watch the clock impatiently waiting for the bell to ring so that I can leave.

I cannot wait until this class is over. It's the only class that really made me feel alone yesterday, and today was worse since I decided to be Mrs. brave. Never again will I do that. How embarrassing. I was straight dissed and pretty much ignored. She was so dry that I can tell she didn't want me near her.

The bell rings and I attend my next classes and have no issues. I greet all of my teachers and wait for everyone to leave after the classes are over to refrain from getting pushed past or shoved while using my walker.

I head to lunch and sit at the table alone awaiting my new-found friend Steven.

I'm wondering if Steven left school early, got sick or just doesn't want to sit with me. I don't see him anywhere. This is very strange, and I have a weird feeling in my gut. I always get these weird gut feelings.

Just as I get worried, I see Steven walking towards the table. He doesn't look too great, something must've happened at home. Maybe I should try to put a smile on his face. I'm not sure how to do that though. I'm pretty new to this friendship business. But I definitely wouldn't want to lose my first friend here at Springville. No way. I better choose my words carefully.

Steven sits down next to me very quietly and doesn't say much, just a simple hello.

"Hey Steven, what took you so long? You let a girl using a walker beat you to the cafeteria? What's that all about?" I said, trying to be sociable and cheer my friend up using humor.

"Well, I'm here now. Just not feeling the best. There was a lot going on at home, and for some reason, the so-called popular kids decided to start raggin on people today. Watch your back." Steven replies.

"What do you mean by raggin? Like making fun of people?" I curiously asked.

"You got it, name calling and chanting. All the dumb stuff that the cool kids get to do without getting in any trouble. They never get caught." Steven says as he looks very disappointed.

"Do you think it's because people are afraid to tell someone that they're giving others a hard time or what?" I asked.

"I don't know," Steven said while shaking his head in shame.

"Well maybe one day they'll stop, or maybe one day someone will speak up. But for now, let's eat some lunch" I said.

"Now you're talking, I'm starved." Says Steven.

"Sorry I'm being dry, just a bad day. Tomorrow will be better or maybe I'll call you later after school when my mood is better. If that's okay of course." says Steven.

"Sounds good to me!" I replied and smiled at my new friend.

Steven and I were eating lunch together, and I spotted that girl Corrine from my class, at another table sitting alone.

"You see that girl over there Steven, the girl sitting all alone?" I asked.

"Ummm yea, that's Corrine. She's always by herself. It's been like that since the first grade." Steven said.

"Well don't you think that's a little odd? I tried speaking to her today in class and she pretty much dissed me with the cold shoulder. Just trying to be nice. I know how it feels to be alone." I said.

"Did you ever stop and think that some people don't want friends? Not saying she doesn't, but maybe she doesn't want to be bothered." Steven said.

I shook my head and continued to eat.

"Is the lunch always this healthy?" I asked with a disappointed look on my face.

Steven and I both laugh together. We actually laugh a lot at each other. I guess that's a good thing.

"I mean don't get me wrong, my mom makes me eat healthy foods at home. She's a health freak, so that's why I was kind of hoping for some unhealthy snacks here at school. Guess not." I explained.

"Well every now and then we get some cookies, brownies and other sweet snacks. I'm actually not really into that stuff. Don't really mind healthy foods. You should be happy that your mom cares so much." Steven replied.

Ring ring ring!

The bell rings indicating that lunch is over and students must go to their next class of the day.

I am starting to feel a little pain throughout my body, but I'll ignore it. The goal is to make it through the day. When I get home, my bed will be waiting for me. It just sucks that no matter how hard I try to be normal, the pains in my body remind me that I'm far from normal. They remind me that I'm sick. I've been sick my entire life basically, but no need for a pity party. Time to get through these classes and hope for the best. I'm looking forward to Stevens call later, I never get calls. Unless it's family.

Now, I am going from class to class feeling sorry for myself. I never felt this way at home. Maybe because at home I am normal. But I've never felt like, sorry for myself until really now. I mean there were times that I felt sad because of pain or not being able to really meet kids my age. Right now, I just feel like going home is best. But would that be letting my condition win? I don't know.

I am sitting in this class taking notes about the solar system. Science is not really my best subject. It's not hard or anything, there just aren't too many topics in science that can keep me awake. Like right now I feel like falling asleep. How embarrassing would that be, especially since mom says that I snore loudly while sleeping. Can you imagine how everyone would laugh at me? What a nightmare! But it is very difficult staying awake in this class. The solar system is boring me to death. Maybe I'm sleepy because I really didn't get any sleep last night. I was so worried about coming to school that my brain kept me up half the night. I even dreamed about coming to school and being alone. It was awful. The day isn't going bad though. It's been fine, so maybe my nerves will chill out.

I leave class to use the restroom. I have to use my walker to get there, but totally refuse to have anyone escort me anywhere. It was recommended, but I'd rather not.

This is my first time using the bathroom here at school, believe it or not. I hope that nobody is in there. It usually takes some effort for me to use the bathroom. The school offered to have the nurse help, but I said no. I need to learn to do things on my own. Plus, I've used the bathroom at home by myself, it's just a matter of moving slowly and not falling down.

Three girls enter the bathroom while I'm still in the stall. Ugh, I left my walker outside of the stall by the sinks, where now the three girls are.

"What's this thing doing in the bathroom, it's taking up all the walking room in this small bathroom," one of the girls said.

"I don't know, but it needs to move. The bathroom isn't big enough for us and that thing. It should've been left outside the bathroom door," Another girl replied.

I am now literally shaking with fear to leave the bathroom because of the mean comments that I'm forced to hear. One of the girls knocks on my door asking me to get out of the bathroom stall. I quickly began to cry, while holding my head. I am also still very much so in physical pain. So right now, I'm being harassed by these girls, while my body is hurting from my condition. This is not my day.

I don't know why these girls decided to do this. All I want to do is come to school, be nice, learn and go back home. I can't say that I am surprised though. I knew it would get worse before it got easy. I keep hearing my mother's voice in my head while they bang, laugh and make mean comments towards me. Suddenly, their voices went away and the door opened and closed. I guess they went back to class. I know my teacher is probably wondering what the heck is taking me so long, even with my disability. Well, I'm going to leave this stall now.

I finally exit the stall and begin to wash and dry my hands. As I leave the bathroom using my walker…

BOOM! Before I knew it, I hit the ground. I had been pushed by one of those mean girls, and they ran. They pushed me down and then ran. My walker is on the ground and so am I.

"Oh my God, oh my God, are you okay? Let me give you a hand and how did this happen?" Mr. Davids asked, the guidance counselor.

I am crying my eyes out, but am very happy to see Mr. Davids again. The first person from Springville to speak to me.

"I was using the bathroom, and these girls came in making fun of my walker while banging on the bathroom door telling me to get out of the stall. Then they left so I thought that it was safe to come out, but it clearly wasn't. I was wrong. As soon as I open the door to leave the bathroom they knocked me down, and here we are now. They pushed me, then ran. I want to go home, please. Please call my parents." I said while crying and sobbing.

Mr. Davids escorts me to the nurse's office, and they call my parents. My parents decide to come get me early from school.

Now I am getting into the car with my mother and father. I'm not too sure how we've come to this so soon. It's only the second day of school for God's sake and I'm already running. Already crying like a baby, and already going home early. Couldn't even make it to October without breaking down. I know that I shouldn't be mad at myself, but I am. Because I knew awful things may happen. Bullying is real. Mean people aren't a myth. Everything I had seen in movies turned out to be real. It was no longer just something I seen on tv. I had been bullied. Now, I must answer all of my parent's questions. This sucks.

"Mya, I am lost for words. Truly I am. Never in a million years would I have thought something like this would even be possible. I am so so sorry." Mom said, while her eyes start to water.

"Mya, you can stay home for a couple days if you'd like. I will also be going up to the school and finding out how this happened. Why doesn't your school have staff on hall duty? This shouldn't have been able to occur. I'm sorry baby girl. My angel. I would do anything for you." Dad said.

"Thanks, guys, I really just rather not say anything right now. I want my bed. That's all I want." I replied.

"Mya, maybe this school thing was a bad idea. Maybe we should reconsider this. It may not be the right time. I'm very concerned." Mom said.

"You're thinking we should pull her?" Dad asked.

"Yes! I cannot and will not deal with cruel kids harming my innocent child. No way. Not my child. She is already suffering, why should she suffer more" Mom said.

"No! I'm staying in school. It was just a bad day. That's all." I said, while tears were still flowing down my face."

My parents were silent and surprised after my little outburst about staying in school. They are really on edge about it all now. This really just sucks man.

I can't believe mom suggested that I just give up. I'm in it now, so I want to go back. This sucks and all, but I also don't miss being in the house all day with grown-ups. Although I was comfortable and didn't have to worry about being knocked to the ground, I wasn't really living life to the fullest at home. I wasn't being a thirteen-year-old. I'm thirteen years old with one friend. That I just met. Never been to a kid's birthday party, football game, or any functions with kids my age. I just need to learn how to make my way around the school. But for now, a warm bath is calling my name. My body was already in pain, so being knocked to the ground really didn't help. That's the plan, bath and relax. Maybe I'll stay home tomorrow, maybe I'll go. It all depends on what cerebral palsy is doing to my body in the morning.

The Iverson house was very quiet. Many thoughts were running through our minds. But, one thing was for sure, my mind was made up. I was not dropping out, instead, I was going back.

Chapter 3

Kicking fears butt: Making my way in.

Today, I am back to school. I've decided to just be a kid. I'm not worrying about what happened to me, I just want to enjoy this as much as I can. I am meeting with Mr. Davids today because of the incident. I guess the school wants to be sure that I'm really okay to be here. Mr. Davids is nice, so I don't mind.

I arrived at Mr. David's office, missing my first two classes of the day. I like Mr. Davids and didn't really care for those two classes so it was no biggie to me.

"Good Morning Mya, how are you feeling today?" asked Mr. Davids.

"I'm alright, how about you?" I replied.

"I'm doing well today, thanks for asking. I really wanted to sit down with you and discuss how you may be feeling after the awful day you had. Again, I'm so sorry that you had to go through all of that. Everyone should be able to feel safe in school. So, I want to work on you feeling safe here at Springville." Mr. Davids said.

"I'm not sure I'll ever feel 100% safe here, but I am sure that I'm not going to give up on being a regular kid. I'm not ready to give up and go back to being homeschooled. Public school is scary, but I wanna try." I replied.

"That is a good attitude to have, but I'd like to change your current opinion on this school. You can feel safe. What happened to you, was a wakeup call to many. But I want to offer you a suggestion. How about getting involved with an organization or school club here? There are plenty of clubs that you can join. It's a good way to make your experience here enjoyable." He said.

"Ummm I don't know about that, I can't even get people to speak to me. I'm not sure how that would go. It may end up being a disaster. I'm taking a break from trying to make friends for a while." I replied.

"I understand that, and I don't want to sound pushy. As your counselor, I'm just letting you know some of your options. There is the book club, math club, science club, theatre club, and a few others. Or you could even start your own if none of these club's interest you at all. I would back you up, and help in any way that I can." He said with lots of energy.

I took a deep breath and gasp. I am trying very hard not to roll my eyes...simply because I really like Mr. Davids. But I really am not in the mood for the conversation that he is trying to have.

"I will think about it, I'm grateful that you're trying to help. I really am." I said.

"I have another suggestion for you Mya. I think you would feel better if you met other kids here that struggle with different disabilities. You are not alone, and meeting other kids with similar conditions will help you through this journey. You are not alone." He said.

"I honestly just want to go to class and get this day over with. Not trying to be rude or anything. I'll consider your suggestions, but right now is not the time. Can I leave now? Please?" I replied.

"Okay, just remember that I am here if you need anything. Even an ear to listen. It's my job and I love my job. You are free to go. I hope you enjoy the rest of your day." He said.

"Thank you," I replied, as I got up and left his office.

I leave my guidance counselors office and heads to my next class period. I am still feeling physically ill and walking is very difficult at the moment. But I am determined to at least attend my classes and make it home. That's the goal, make it through the day.

I think that what's bothering me right now more than anything is the physical pain that I have. Cerebral Palsy can really get a girl down. There are four different types of cerebral Palsy, but the one I have is called spastic cerebral palsy. This basically makes my body stiff as rocks. Imagine walking and your entire body just stiffening up on you. Sucks. Enough of my pity party, I see my one and only friend that I have here. He spotted me, as I spotted him. Steven Roberts.

"Mya Mya Mya!!" Steven yelled from down the hall.

"Steven Steven Steven!!" I yelled back.

Steven sprints down the hall towards me, screaming wait!

"Mya, oh my God Mya. I heard what happened, so wish I was there so that I could have helped you and put those bullies in their places. You are such a cool person, that shouldn't have happened. What jerks. Are you okay?" He asked.

"I just got finished speaking with the guidance counselor about this, I'm done with it. Thank you though." I replied, appearing very annoyed.

"Look who is coming our way Mya, that girl Corrine who sits alone at lunch." He said as Corrine walked up to me.

"Hey, Mya, is it?" Corrine asked.

"Yeah," I replied, super confused and annoyed.

"Well, uh, I just wanted to tell you that I heard what happened and that was messed up. Maybe we could talk sometime." Corrine said.

I'm thinking to myself that this girl cannot be serious. I literally went out of my way to try and be friends. But now that she feels sorry for me we can be friends. I'm one big joke around here. Just what I didn't want to happen is happening. People are feeling obligated to feel sorry for me. But why make an enemy?

"Yeah, we should. Definitely" I agreed.

"Well that was interesting, wasn't it?" Steven sarcastically asked.

"Yes, it was. Very strange. I don't want anyone to be my friend because they feel sorry for me. That is not a real friend." I said.

"Don't judge a book by its cover Mya." He replied.

"I am always the one judged. It's never the other way around." I replied.

"Don't you think you judged her, and approached her because you felt pity? You assumed because she sits alone that she must be lonely and in need of friends. I smell judging!" He said, with a smirk on his face.

I laughed for the first time all day. Steven seems to have brought sunshine to my day.

"You're right. You got that." I replied, after several laughs.

"Well I think we should get going to class and I'll see you at lunch" I said.

"Okay see ya later," he replied.

I just want to laugh like that every day. What he said about me being judgy of Corrine wasn't even that funny, but anything funny is worth a hard laugh from me. I use to laugh and smile all the time before school began. Steven doesn't even bombard me with a million questions about my illness, most people I come across do. It's strange. Why is he such a good friend? A thought that won't leave my brain, but for now, he's my good friend. My first and only friend so far.

I went to my next classes on my schedule making it on time to each. I am so exhausted from the walking back and forth. It is taking a toll on my body because I'm not used to moving and walking this much yet. But I will be, hopefully.

"Knock Knock." Someone knocks and comes into my class.

"Ms. Iverson, your mother is on the phone for you in the main office."

I should've known my mom would call. She was worried this morning when bringing me to school. I can't exactly be mad at her, but doesn't she get that this is embarrassing. Not to mention, I have to walk all the way to the main office and back just to tell her that I'm okay. I'm going to see her every day after school, she should just wait until then.

"Hey, mom, what's up? I asked, and grunted.

"Love, you know that we are very worried about you. I just had to check in to make sure that you were okay. How are you feeling? You know that we can always come and get you at any time." Mom said.

"I am just really tired. But mom, please stop calling. I'll see you at home. Love you." I said.

"I love you too Mya, my love." Mom replied.

Sometimes I wonder, maybe my parents didn't make the best choice by keeping me home from school all of these years. I'm a social dub and a complete outsider here. I'm in a totally different world with no idea how to fit in. I really hope mom and dad take me shopping. I'm really looking forward to getting new clothes. Better than what I always wear. My parents always offered to take me shopping, but I stay home all the time so why get new clothes. Totally different case now. I'm dressed like a grandma compared to these other girls. I don't even have earrings. I guess that sums up my dreads. I thought they'd make me less like a grandma. Dad was furious. Mom didn't really have much to say. So many things run through my brain now, that I've never even thought about before.

Like Steven, is he just a really nice person? Does he want to be friends, or does he have a crush on me? Sometimes the way he looks at me makes me believe that he has a crush on me. But again. I'm new to all of this and probably am over thinking. Why would he want to be with a girl who sometimes can barely walk? I'm not sure I would if the shoe was on the other foot. But who knows.

I am halfway through my day, and now I am heading to lunch. I am anxious to see my friend and finally eat something. I'm starving.

So, I get to the cafeteria, and Steven is already there waiting for me. Well, at least it looks like he's waiting for me. He beat me to the table this time. He's sitting there with a bright smile, cheesing super hard. Maybe he thinks I'm all depressed about being pushed to the ground when really, I'm over It. I don't want anyone trying to "cheer me up." Or maybe he's just in a really good mood today.

"Hello there, you beat me to the table this time. Let's get in line for food." I said to Steven.

"Yeah, I wanted to hear about your day so far! The day is almost over. Totally wish we had classes together. Having a friend this year is going to be great." Steven replied.

"Aww, thanks, Steven. My day has been pretty chill, other than my mom calling me on the main office phone. She just called to see how I was, but that could've waited. How has your day been going? This lunch line is kind of long, hope it moves fast. I'm starved." I said.

"My day has been the same as any other day I guess ha-ha...and yeah. The line is long, but today is pizza! My favorite. It'll be worth the wait." He said.

"Look who is walking towards us once again," I said.

"Oh shoot, its Corrine again. This is strange. She usually never even comes into the lunch line. She is always bringing lunch from home and eating alone. Maybe she's over that loner life. I mean, I'm a loner too. But Corrine invented the term loner. Seriously." He replied.

Corrine slowly walks near me and Steven. She appears to want to talk, but is afraid. I am a little annoyed by her, but I will try my best to shake It off, Steven is pretending to not even see her.

"Well, here she comes. Let's be nice," I said, while giving Steven a look.

"Hi," Corrine said.

"Hey what's up Corrine." Steven and I said at the same time.

"Mya, I was wondering if we could forget about class," Corrine said.

"What do you mean?" I said.

"Ya know. When you tried to talk to me. It wasn't a good day for me. I really didn't want to talk to anyone, well I usually don't. But can we forget about it? You were just trying to be nice, and I treated you how everyone else treats me." Corrine said.

"Yeah, we're cool. No worries. I have bigger things to worry about. Ya know like not being pushed down ha-ha, or ya know cerebral palsy kicking my butt." I said while laughing.

Steven and Corrine stare each other not knowing if I was actually joking or being sarcastic. So, they just don't respond to my comment at all.

"So, have you guys ever spoken before? This is my first time going to public school so I need to catch up on everything. Who liked who, whose kissed, who hates each other, and who are the best friend groups." I said.

"We've never really spoken, just seen her around," Steven said.

"Yeah, and I have no idea about those other things you mentioned." Corrine said.

"I mean, everyone is just really weird around here. Sadly, you've already met the Springville bullies. They've been that way since forever. It sucks that they always get away with everything." Steven said.

"Not for too much longer. Something has got to give. I may be a cripple, but I'm tough." I replied to Steven with confidence.

"I just keep to myself, and try to stay out of people's way," Corrine said.

The three of us sit together at the lunch table in the cafeteria after receiving our food.

"We should all hang out at my house after school. If you want. We could order food, watch a movie, do homework, or whatever." I suggested.

"I'm down," Steven replied with excitement.

"What about you Corrine?" I asked.

"Are you sure you want me there? At your house?" Corrine asked.

"Yeah, why not? I'm not mad about the classroom. Cheers to a new start." I said.

"Cheers with milk cartoons. Cool ha-ha." Steven said.

"So, what do you say Corrine? Coming?" I asked.

"Sure. Why not." Corrine replied.

"Cool. My first guest ever, besides my family members but they don't count." I said, smiling.

"Well, we'll be there. Just write down your address on this piece of paper." Steven replied.

As I write down my address for Steven and Corrine, the bell rings for the ending of lunch. I give them the address and head to my next class.

"Do you need any help getting to class Mya?" Steven asked.

"Nah, I'm good. Thanks, Steven." I replied.

Steven took off running because his class is pretty far from the cafeteria and he is usually late to class.

My day is almost over and now I'm starting to think about Mr. Davids. He was really trying to show me some love, and I basically dissed him. I think I should maybe go back to his office. His suggestions weren't bad, I just wasn't really in the mood to listen or talk. My day is almost over now, but tomorrow I'll visit him again. I've been thinking about some of his suggestions, and I may consider.

Depending on how the next few days, or couple of weeks go. I didn't come to Springville to be a hermit crab. I didn't come to just go to class and go back home. In that case, I could've just stayed home. But to be honest, I was getting really lonely at home. My parents are cool, the coolest ever.

But that just wasn't enough anymore. I'm not a baby anymore. Next year I'll be a freshman in high school, then I'll be in college somewhere. The world outside my home is different, but I gotta grow up eventually. Why not start now. My grandmother always says that I have an old soul. She thinks I've always been mature for my age, and that talking to me was like talking to someone who was "here" before. She claimed there was something different about me, other than my disability.

I guess I should pay more attention to my teacher, rather than my own personal thoughts. I can't help it though. Sitting in a classroom is quite boring. And it's really cold in each classroom. I guess a jacket will be needed. Time does seem to be going by fast. I don't carry my cell phone on me while I'm in class. My way of being studious, I guess. I wish that I had it on me right about now. But, I want to make my family proud. Not by just being social, but also my grades. This would be the first time that mom and dad wait for a report card to come in the mail. Should be interesting…hope I do well. I did well with homeschooling, hopefully it'll be the same.

My teacher just handed me a take-home assignment to do. Wow, actual homework. Weirdly, I'm excited about this. Makes me feel normal. When I go home, I'll shower and get started right away. I probably won't be excited about homework after a while ha-ha. On tv, all the kids usually hate doing their homework. It's funny that everything I watched on tv and wished for is actually happening. I'm not sure if this is good or bad but it's happening. I'm finally getting to see what it's like to go to school, and experience life outside of my parents. Even after being teased, and pushed to the ground, I'm still glad I chose to come to school. I finally feel like a thirteen-year-old. Finally.

Chapter 4

Still making my way: The Creation of The Unpretty Project

Finally, I am home after a long day of classes. My day went pretty well though. No bullies and no being pushed down. And I made another friend. I'd say today was a success. Oh, and they're coming over today to hang out. My first friends over ever. I have to tell mom! She's going to be so happy for me. Finally, I have friends.

"Hey mom, I invited two new friends over today. I hope that's alright with you and dad." I said.

"Friends, How many?" Mom asked.

"Just two, Steven and Corrine," I replied.

"Wow, this is exciting, right? Of course, it's okay. I'll just run it by your dad, but I'm sure that he'll be ecstatic. Our baby making friends. Go, girl." Mom said, in excitement.

I knew mom would overreact. It's really not that big of a deal honestly. Just two people I met in school, and we happened to start talking. Mom probably thinks were already like BFFS. Ha-ha, well not yet. Maybe one day. I always wanted a BFF to hang out with, and share secrets with. I have no siblings and until now, I had no friends. But ya know, life wasn't all that bad. Lonely at times, but I guess I should be grateful for my parents. I don't think Steven has the best parents. He hasn't really shared many details, yet. But I'm sure he will.

"Honey, your dad wants to know what time your friends are coming." Mom said.

"Ummm we didn't really set a time. I just gave them my phone number and address." I replied.

"Well, next time get a time hon, and maybe give us more of a heads up. Just so we can prepare and make your friends welcomed here." Mom said.

"No problem mom, right now I'll just wait for their phone call or knock on the door," I replied.

"Okay, Mya. Are you happy?" Mom asked.

"Yeah, don't make a huge deal out of this alright." I asked nicely.

Ring Ring Ring!

The phone is ringing and I immediately got so nervous. I immediately assume that they are at the door, or canceling on me. That would totally suck.

"Mya are you going to answer your phone." Mom said.

"Yes, mom. It's probably Steven or Corrine." I nervously replied.

"Hello?" I said when answering my cell phone.

"Hey, what took you so long. We called twice. You going deaf?" Steven said over the phone to me.

"Sorry. What's up?" I replied, nervously.

"Ummm did you forget we all had plans to hang out at your place? I think were outside your front door. Don't tell me you're flaking on us." Steven said.

"Wow, that was quick. I'll be at the door in a minute." I said.

I can't believe they got here so quickly. That was beyond fast. I've only been home for less than an hour. Good thing I'm dressed or even home. Usually, mom likes to stop at the grocery store before going home but we didn't today.

"Mom, my friends are here. Just letting you know." I said.

"Okay, honey I want to meet these friends, but don't worry. I won't pry. Just want to say hello. I'm sure your dad wants to meet them as well." Mom said.

"Ryan, Ryan come downstairs and meet Mya's new friends. Hurry honey." Mom yelled out to dad.

"Oh, Oh alright. Be down in one sec." Dad replied with excitement.

Me and my mom walk to the front door to let my friends inside of our house.

"Hey, come in." I said.

"Welcome. Make yourself at home. We are so glad you guys decided to come by and hang out with Mya." Mom said.

Dad finally comes downstairs to greet my guest.

"Hey, I'm Mr. Iverson, and you've already met my wife Mrs. Iverson. Obviously ha-ha. Please feel at home. My home is your home." Dad said.

Steven and Corrine both said thank you to my parents and followed me to our basement. Our basement is pretty cool because we have like a rec room. I come down here all the time to watch movies or catch up on my favorite shows.

"So, what do you guys wanna do first? I was thinking Netflix, homework, and order some pizza? With hot wings?"

"I'm down for whatever," Corrine said.

"Yep me too," Steven said.

This is going to be very awkward for me. I'm not really exactly sure how to be a good host. I don't want them to feel bored because then they won't come back and I like having friends. I hope my suggestion wasn't too lame. Food and Netflix are always my favorite things to do. Well, l I guess they are the only things I do. Such a lame I guess. Maybe I'm being too hard on myself. I'll ask them to pick the movie or whatever show.

"So, what do you guys like on your pizza? I'm just a regular cheese type of person. Every now and then pepperoni." I said.

"I really don't want the pizza, but I'll eat some wings," Corrine said.

"I'll have pepperoni Mya, thanks. Now let's get this party started. No awkwardness allowed. The three amigos." Steven said while smiling hard.

We all started smiling and laughing. There is a feeling of safety and friendship in the room. My mom orders food, as we take out our homework assignments and turn Netflix on.

"Well, since we are all new friends, maybe we should start this hang out session by getting to know each other a little more," I said.

"Agreed." Both Steven and Corrine said.

"So how about we start with Springville. Mya, you've only been there for like a hot second, what do you think about it? Aside from those jerks." Steven asked.

"Well, really. I don't know…" I replied.

"I mean, like do you wish you'd never even came to Springville? Is it a total disaster?" Corrine asked.

"It's going to be kinda hard to talk about my experience at Springville so far while ignoring the fact that I was pushed to the grown by a group of wanna be mean girls," I said.

We all started laughing like we've known each other for years.

"Don't worry, one day we'll get em," Steven replied while still laughing.

"I don't wanna get em, I just don't want to be bothered by them again," I said.

"An apology would be nice," I added.

"Hmm, wishful thinking," Steven said sarcastically while rolling his eyes.

"So, Corrine…what has life been like for you at Springville?" I asked.

"Now this is going to be a sticky answer for me..do I have to share?" Corrine asked.

"YES, we are all going to share. Come on Corrine." Steven said.

"Well, it hasn't been all that great. But maybe it could be worse somewhere else. Teachers are alright. They don't really go out of their way but they're fine. Students are jerks, and pretty much have made my life hell since elementary days." Corrine said.

"Is that why you don't talk to anyone in school, ever? And you sit alone at lunch?" I asked.

"Nobody usually tries to talk to me, it's as if I'm not even there. So that's just the way it is at school. When you tried to talk to me, I was already having a bad day and It caught me totally off guard." Corrine said.

"I don't really care anymore now. Like, about having friends or whatever. You guys are cool though." Corrine said.

"It really sucks how so much bullying happens at our school, and I feel too crippled to do anything about it," I replied.

"There would be no point anyway. These kids even have teachers wrapped around their fingers. Popularity rules." Steven said.

"Well not anymore…I mean why should we stand for it? I know eventually they'll try to bother me again. So why should I wait for it to happen." I said.

Knock knock! My mom comes into the basement room to bring us pizza, wings, and soda.

So, how's it going guys? Mom asked.

"Fine," All three of us said at the same time.

"Alright, I hope you all are enjoying yourselves. Mya did you tell them we have a bunch of movies, and board games?" Mom asked.

"Mom, I've got it," I said.

"Well alright, Mya. You guys enjoy the food." Mom said.

Mom leaves us be, and heads back upstairs.

"Mmmm, this food smells so good, I'm ready to dive in." Steven said.

"Well let's dig in. Then we should probably get some homework done ha-ha." I said.

"But wait, Mya, finish what you were telling us before your mom came down," Corrine said.

"I have an idea, that's all," I replied.

"Ummm a plan?" Steven replied while looking at me like I was crazy.

"Yes, a plan," I said and continued to eat my food.

"You know for a crippled girl you have a lot of guts," Corrine said.

"Crippled? Really?" Steven said.

"So, we are going to be sensitive? I'm just kidding around." Corrine said.

"Yeah, it's cool. I've got pretty tough skin believe it or not." I said.

"Heck yeah you do, most people wouldn't have even come back to school," Steven said.

"We still don't know what this plan is of yours," Corrine said.

"Well, I really wasn't going to share until I was sure. My parents don't even know. It's just an idea really." I said.

"Come on, share. We are the new three amigos." Steven said while laughing.

"Well, you know our guidance counselor? Mr. Davids?" I asked.

"Uhm yeah," Steven replied.

"Yeah, what about him?" Corrine replied.

"Well, he was telling me that I should join an organization or club at Springville to get to know people, not be bored at school, and basically so I can feel less like a stranger when I'm there. Like I don't belong. He's a pretty cool guy. He was the first person to even speak to me at Springville." I said.

"Sooo, your idea to stop those bullies is to join some club at school.?" Corrine replied, with a confused look on her face.

"Yeah, ugh cool idea but I doubt that will have any impact on those wannabe girls." Steven said.

"No, that's not my idea exactly. None of the clubs at Springville sound like anything I want to be a part of. They sound pretty dull and boring." I replied.

"So, what the heck is your idea? And what does it have to do with what Mr. Davids said to you?" Steven replied.

"Spill the beans already," Corrine said.

"Well, alright. Since none of his club ideas really interest me, I decided to start my own." I said.

"Start your own school club at Springville? Really?" Steven said.

"This is definitely random, not a bad idea but random," Corrine said.

"I really think that this could be a good thing. Tell us more. What kind of group will it be?" Steven said.

"I think it could be a good idea as well. I just don't think anything will get to those jerks." Corrine said.

"I'm not even sure if I'm really going to do it guys, just an idea. I'll talk to Mr. Davids tomorrow. But it would be a group for kids who need a friend, especially kids with some sort of disability like me. Mr. Davids said that there are so many kids like me at Springville. I'd like to get us all together. Why not.. Oh, and maybe this group could do like some community service activities. I was also thinking it could be an all-girls group. Sorry Steven ha-ha." I said.

"Well, way to count me out. But this sounds like a cool idea. Why not just try." Steven said.

"The group would be called, The Unpretty Project. Just something I thought of. It would basically describe how so many of us girls feel every day." I said.

"I'm in, I'll be apart. But how does this tie into those bullies?" Corrine asked.

"Because this group would let everyone see how they are treating people. We will bring attention to the bullying epidemic in our school...told ya I had tough skin. Can't fight physically, but I can fight with my brain." I said.

I guess we don't give ourselves a pat on the back when we needed, but I'm proud of myself for even considering this idea. I've always done community service with my parents and other family members growing up. I've always wanted a sister, so this group will give me like several sisters. I hope Steven and Corrine aren't thinking I'm totally crazy for this. But I think this will be a good thing...

"Tomorrow I'll go to Mr. Davids office to get an approval to start this group. Who says the crippled girl can't be active around Springville? Ha-ha." I said sarcastically while laughing.

"I almost forgot that you have cerebral palsy," Steven said.

"Well, my body reminds me every day," I said.

Mom comes downstairs to check on us.

"Everything alright guys? Just checking in." Mom said.

"Fine!" All three of us said loudly.

"Sounds like I'm unwelcomed." Mom said.

"Na, Mrs. Iverson. Everything's fine, you're welcome to join us if you'd like..." Steven said.

"Well, how sweet of you. But I wouldn't want to be in the way of you kiddos. I'll be upstairs if you guys need anything." Mom said.

"Your mom is awesome Mya," Corrine said.
"Ditto. She's so cool," Steven said.

"I guess I should be more grateful. She tried her best to make me feel like the opposite of, an Unpretty Project. But somethings parents just can't control how we feel, and it's not their fault. I can't wait to tell her about my idea though. I'm sure she will be super proud. I'm so happy you guys came over, let's watch Netflix now." I said.

Tomorrow will begin a new chapter for me at Springville. Something to look forward to.

Chapter 5

The crippled girl is in town, make room

The next day at school,

Yesterday was fun, my first time to have friends over. Before Steven, and Corrine left we played a couple games of Uno. I won both games, I'm like a pro at Uno. We also watched a couple movies on Netflix. There were no pizza or wings left, but that's fine. I'm sure mom didn't want any. It was cool, I guess this is what it's like to be a regular teenager and have some sort of social life. Steven seems to be a friend that I'll have for a long time, but I'm not quite sure about Corrine. She spoke yesterday and shared a few laughs but she was still very distant in a way. Maybe it's too early, and that'll change. Who knows. But today, I have to worry about other things.

I am meeting with my guidance counselor again for two reasons. He wants to follow up with me about everything that happened, and I want to tell him about my idea. I hope he likes it, or at least will give it a shot. I've never really started anything on my own. Oh wait, there are three reasons I'm going to see him. The last reason would be to apologize. I was really rude during our last meeting, but that's just because everything had just happened. I was over it all. So, this should be a good meeting today.

Mr. Davids said that I can come to his office first thing in the morning if I wanted. I guess I shouldn't keep missing my first period class, but this is important. One more time won't hurt me.

I walked to Mr. Davids office, and the secretary tells me to wait for him because he's not there. While sitting there, I notice that there are so many pictures of students that appeared to have some form of disability hung up on his wall. Very interesting, and yet strange at the same time.

I wonder if he has a thing for handicapped kids. It's sorta weird. Maybe weird is the wrong word to use. Maybe he's helped all these students on his wall. I wonder if they all go to Springville, I haven't seen any of these faces yet.

Mr. Davids walks in with a bright smile, happy to see me.

"Good Morning Mya, how are you?" Mr. Davids asked.

"Morning, I'm doing much better, feeling good this morning. How are you, Mr. Davids?" I asked.

"I'm doing excellent, couldn't be better Mya." Mr. Davids replied.

"Man, you really love your job, don't you? You really love Springville..." I said.

"Well, yes I do. For sure. There's nothing else I rather do." Mr. Davids said.

"Wait a minute, maybe I'd be a Broadway singer ha-ha, but I'd never get passed the audition." Mr. Davids said jokingly.

"Well, ya never know Mr. Davids. Go for it. You may get lucky." I said.

"Maybe. But, was there anything that you wanted to speak to me about specifically or were you just coming by to greet the greatest counselor in the world?" Mr. Davids asked.

"You are a pretty darn good counselor, and I'm about to tell you why," I said.

"This outta be good. I'm listening. All ears." Mr. Davids said.

"Okay well, here it goes. Remember you suggested that I join a school club or organization? Well, I wasn't really interested in any of the ones that you suggested. No offense. But, I did decide to start my own." I said with excitement.

"WOW, I think that's a great idea. Can you explain to me what kind of club you would like to start? Any details? This is very good news!" Mr. Davids asked, smiling hard.

"So, glad you asked Mr. Davids, well I want to start a group for girls who struggle with disabilities like myself. Girls who get bullied, or don't have many friends. Boys can come to meetings if they want to…but this is really for girls. I feel like I should be doing something at this school, especially since I just got here. So why not start my own club that interests me. What do you think?" I asked.

"This all sounds really good, but I have one question." Mr. Davids asked.

"Ummm shoot." I curiously replied.

"What are you going to call this awesome girl group? Does it have a name yet?" Mr. David asked.

"Oh, of course! I'm going to call it, The Unpretty Project. Do you like it? The name kinda represents how my Cerebral Palsy makes me feel." I said.

"A unique name, I like it. So, do you have any plans? How can I help? And when will you be ready to get started?" Mr. Davids asked.

"Well, so far I just want to get flyers made, have like some sort of meeting and then collect warm clothing for the homeless. That will be the kick-off of The Unpretty Project. Maybe we can pass out flyers in the café, and have a table set up for donations. You know, like hats, gloves, and scarves. Whatcha think?" I asked.

"Let's get started, you work on the flyers and I'll get permission for them to be put up on the halls. Also, I will work on getting an okay to use the café for your hat, glove, and scarf drive. Sound good?" Mr. Davids asked.

"Perfecto," I responded.

"Okay you should get to class now, thanks for coming by and I'm so excited for you! Way to make an effort." Mr. Davids said.

"Thank ya for the inspiration, see ya later! Oh, and sorry about the other day. I was pretty frustrated." I replied as I walked out of the door.

I feel really good about my decision to start this group. I don't want to be one of those students who have no friends, so they do absolutely nothing. I don't want my disability to stop me from doing stuff in school, being active or involved. I can't play sports, so I need to find my way. I'm slowly but surely finding my way.

Now it's time to go to class and be a student. I'm not really worried about the work aspect of school. That probably doesn't make any sense. But I'm pretty good with the books. I guess because my head has always been in the books, and nothing else. Literally. But, I still need to balance the books with whatever social activities I will be a part of.

I am sitting in this boring class listening to my teacher lecture and go on and on. When I first entered the class nobody spoke to me, but they all stared. Not surprised at all. The stares don't bother me because I am used to it. But I'm wondering how people will react to my new idea. Maybe they will like it and realize I am not just a weirdo. Maybe.

"Mya, are you awake?" The teacher asked.

"Ummm, yes," I replied.

Why did she ask me that? My eyes weren't even closed. I'm confused. Does it look like I'm not listening or something? I don't know.
Although, I am deep in my own thoughts. I am still listening to her.

About forty-five minutes go by of long, boring mathematical breakdowns. Finally, the teacher hands out classwork assignments for everyone to complete, and if we don't finish it will be homework. This is the part of the class that I do not look forward to. I would prefer her to continue teaching then stop and ask us to work together on assignments. Nobody in any of my classes really speaks to me. They assume I'm brain dead or something because I have a walker. Idiots. That wasn't nice of me, but oh well.

"Mya, may I see you for a second." The teacher asked.

I'm kinda tired of people asking if they can see me for a second. I'm totally over it. Because I know that they only want to talk about my disability, getting bullied by those girls, or not really being social in class. It's just getting annoying especially since I just got here. Give me a break. Starting this group will really show people that I'm not trying to be a weirdo. I want to be normal. Although my grandmother always told me that I'm not normal. She always said I'm special and one day I'll know why. Whatever that means. I hope special doesn't mean weird.

"Yes?" I responded.

"I just wanted to ask you how you are." The teacher asked.

"Oh thanks, I'm fine." I responded.

"How are you liking our school so far?" The teacher asked.

"It's school, I guess," I said. I shrugged my shoulders, and walked away.

As the day goes by, I am so anxious to get home so that I can start getting things together for the group.

My day has been pretty long, I'm actually feeling weak but I don't care. I'm ready to start my new project. After school, I'm going to work on flyers. I could actually get dad to help me. I forgot that my dad is pretty good with that stuff.

My mom picked me up from school, curious about a few things, well actually she's curious about everything! Of course.

"So, Mya," Mom said in a weird voice of curiosity.

"Yes mom," I answered.

"Are you sure these new friends of yours are actually good friends?" Mom asked.

"Yes, mom they are great so far. They're the only people that I actually talk to besides my guidance counselor. He's great." I replied.

"Okay honey, I'm really just always worried about you. I want you to know that I love you so much. Never forget that. And your dad loves you too." Mom said.

"I know mom, and I love you guys too. But you have to let me live a little. I'm not a baby. I know I have cerebral palsy, but you know I'm doing way better than most. I'm a tough girl. I'm ready to fully be a Springville student." I exclaimed.

When I got home I immediately called Steven and Corrine to see if they could come over to hang out and help me out with my new idea. I keep forgetting to tell my mom about my idea. I guess I should. She's going to like it, but a thousand questions will probably come that I don't feel like answering. As always.

"Mom, I called my friends to come over so they can help me with an activity that I'm starting at school. It's no big deal, just something to get me more active. I'm starting a girls group. It'll be for girls like me, I guess." I said, trying to keep it short with her.

"Wow, this is new. Am I the last to know? I guess you really are growing up. Well congrats, I kinda think it is a big deal. You haven't even been in school for a month and so much is happening. I'm proud of you." Mom said.

"Thank you, mom," I said.

"Just please keep me in the loop, I want us to stay close how we are. Even if you are in school." Mom said, with a sad expression on her face.

"Don't worry mom. You'll always be my number one friend." I said, and winked at my loving, overprotective mother.

"So, are your friends coming?" Mom asked.

"Yes, but you don't need to order us food again or anything." I said.

"Alright, I will. Just let me know if you guys need anything. I'm so happy with your progress. I'm going to take a nap, your mom is exhausted." Mom said.

"Okay mom, we'll keep it down," I said.

So now, I'm going to chill out and wait for them to come. It's pretty cool being able to do that. Before school, there were times when I'd be so bored at home. I would just dream of having at least one friend to call, or chill with. Being alone is cool sometimes, but not all the time. And that's how my life was. Hanging out with your mom gets played out.

I've been so caught up with school, fitting in, and making friends that I haven't really been keeping track of my health. I need to make sure I see my nurse and do my exercises. I also have medication and vitamins to take, that I've been forgetting to take. I guess that's why I haven't been feeling the best. I guess I need to learn how to balance my new life.

Knock knock!

I guess that's them. They get here pretty fast.

"Hey guys, come in. How did you get here?" I said.

"My mom brought us. We don't live too far, and I'm sure she's happy to get me out of the house." Steven said.

"So, what do you wanna do?" Corrine and Steven both asked me.

"I want you guys to help me make a flyer. The flyer will be for The Unpretty Projects first meeting and that we will be collecting hats, gloves, and scarves." I said.

"Oh cool, where will the meeting be?" Steven asked.

"Well, I'm hoping after school in the cafeteria. So, we can just put that on the flyer. Mr. Davids is going to get the cafeteria approved for us." I said.

"I don't even know why I asked since, I'm not invited. Since it's all girls allowed." Steven said.

"Whatever Steven, you can still help a friend," I said in a sharp tone.

"I'm pretty good with the computers and designing things. I'll give it a try if you have a laptop." Corrine said.

"And I'll give my brilliant ideas too, for a fee….just kidding," Steven said.

I go upstairs to get my laptop, and then we began to work on the flyer. I am so happy that my new friends came and are willing to help me out with this new idea.

"What colors do you want to use on the flyers, Mya? Ms. Lady in charge. Ms. Kicking cerebral palsy's butt." Steven said.

"Ha-ha stop it. Sometimes it kicks my butt, and I'm no lady in charge. But, I like purple and black. I think it'll be cute. Or even white letters." I said.

"Hmmm okay, we'll work it out. It'll be perfect." Corrine said.

"Maybe we could even put a picture of a group of girls on the front? I don't know, just trying to be creative." Steven said.

"Not a bad idea, you guys are the best. Really." I said with joy.

"You know guys, I have to be honest. Nobody speaks to me in any of my classes. Why in the world would they come to this meeting or donate anything? I'm the crippled loser in all of my classes." I said.

"Well, that makes three of us," Steven said.

I started to shake my head and laugh at the same time. Steven can be difficult to take seriously. He's a comedian in his own right.

"Yeah seriously, that makes three of us. You know I'll be at the meeting. Speaking of, what date are we putting on this flyer?" Corrine asked.

"Ummm, how about next Monday, after school? I saw on the board in the main office that there are no activities or meetings going on, so let's go with that. I'll show Mr. Davids the flyer, and he can tell me if it'll be okay. If not we can always go into the computer and change the date." I said.

"I'm proud of you. Doing something that matters, and you've been here for less than a month. Maybe you can be school president one day. Who knows." Steven said.

"I agree, Vote for Iverson. Sounds good. I'll be your secretary. For a small rate." Corrine added. "You guys…stop it." I said, while blushing.

"Take a look at what I have done so far, and umm are you feeding us for all this hard work?" Corrine asked, with a smirk on her face.

"Oh, my goodness, Corrine..well I can't lie, food is on my mind too ha-ha," Steven said.

"Well, I can grab some snacks from upstairs real quick, then look at the flyer. Greedy monsters. You guys keeping coming over, our fridge will probably end up being empty." I said.

I went goes upstairs and grabbed Oreos, kool-aid jammers, nachos and cheese, and left-over quesadillas that my mom made for dinner the previous night.

"Here, go crazy. Eat it all," I said.

"Well, thank you. This is good hospitality," Steven said.

"Okay, let me see the flyer now," I said.

"Here ya go," Corrine said.

"OH, my!! It's perfect. The words pop, the flyer is super girly and has lots of purples, which is my favorite color." I said with excitement.

Steven and Corrine got picked up by Stevens mother. I printed out a couple copies of the flyer that they created, to show Mr. Davids. I am really hoping that by the next day everything will be approved so that I can spend my entire weekend preparing for her first big meeting.

With A Little Magic.

Chapter 6

Everyone needs a little break, right?

So, it's the weekend, well it's Friday. My guidance counselor said that the principal approved the group, the meeting, and the drive. This is great news, right? Well, why has the excitement kinda left me? I don't feel happy like, I should be. It's just fear maybe. Again, worrying about people showing up or liking the idea. I just want to help people who feel how I feel almost 90% of the time. Feeling Unpretty is a state of mind that I'm almost always in. I can't even totally blame Cerebral Palsy. It's just everything about me, hasn't really given me much confidence. Until now. I felt some confidence when I decided to stay in school after being pushed to the ground and feeling helpless. Then coming up with this idea made me feel good too. But the feeling doesn't last. I wonder when it will. I'd like to feel confident all the time, but does anyone? These are things I wanna talk to other girls about. I feel like I've just missed so much. But I guess it's too late to chicken out now. I'm the tough cripple girl. I guess.

A part of me feels like maybe things have escalated too quickly. I've already had friends over my house two days in a row, and now this group. It's a lot. But I've always had ideas in my head, and a big imagination. School is kinda giving me the room to express these things. But being afraid is something that I simply cannot hide. I speak and act older than everyone else because I'm always around adults. I walk and speak differently.

What's the real use in trying to just "fit in," it'll be almost a waste of time? I sometimes pray and ask God to completely cure me of Cerebral Palsy because that's my biggest issue. I hear words in my head perfectly fine, but then when I go to speak to others it comes out sounding weird. Not all the time, but a lot of times. My mind is rambling and rambling. So many things to think about. My biggest question is, am I wasting my time in Springville? Eighth grade is a late start in the game.

Today I plan to buy a few outfits with my mom. I haven't spent much time with her lately, and I do feel somewhat bad. She's been there for me my whole life, and I haven't really spent any time with her or spoken to her. Going shopping will be perfect because my mom is super girly, and loves buying new clothes. I think I'm going to get an outfit specifically for Monday since I'm having my first meeting. Mom will really enjoy helping me out with that. I guess today will be a mother, daughter day. She will probably ask me more questions about my new friends and school. I hope not. Mom worries too much.

I'm actually not feeling good so I may ask to see my nurse or make a doctor's appointment. I could be just tired. Who knows.

Later that day around 6 pm, I went into my mom's room to ask if we could head to the mall to go shopping. As I was walking up the stairs to my mom's room I started to feel a little dizzy and my legs began to feel very tight. I am assuming it is because of all the new walking that I've been doing at school now. My body is adjusting.

"Oh, my goodness, are you okay? Come sit down. What's wrong?" Dad asked in his worried voice.

My dad saw me really struggling to get up the stairs. Usually, I can get up there with no problem, it just takes me some time. But right now, I am bent over, basically forcing myself up the stairs.

"Honey, come downstairs! I think we may need to call Mya's nurse or take her to the hospital." Dad yelled.

"Mya, oh my God." Mom cried.
"I'm fine you guys, just a bit tired," I replied.

"No, I'm thinking maybe you need to rest this weekend and take a few days off from school to see a doctor. And we can call your nurse over too." Mom said.

"Umm no mom, I can't miss school Monday. I have to go. I'm fine. You guys are just overreacting. I have cerebral palsy. Sometimes I will have pain. Sometimes walking will be tough. It's my reality, and it's been my reality since birth. The only difference now is my schedule." I said while crying.

"Calm down Mya, we won't take you out of school," Dad said.

"We won't?" Mom asked in a sarcastic voice.

"No, but you do need to get back on top of your health. Your health comes first. The minute you stop keeping up with your health, we will have no choice, but to have you homeschooled again. And you will be taking a few days off from school just to get back on track." Dad said.

"Alright, but just not Monday. I really need to be in school on Monday Dad. Really." I yelled, in tears.

"Fine Mya, but then you'll be home," Dad said.

My mom is still crying because she's so distraught about her daughter being in pain. She really wants me to go back to homeschooling because she's terrified of me being in any pain. She is also still upset about me getting bullied at school. My mom feels that there is just too much happening, way too fast.

"Mom stop crying, alright. I'm tough remember?" I said.

Me and my parents all smile at each other and hug.

"Mom, I really want to go shopping tonight. Is that still a possibility? I really want to go. Like really." I said.

"I don't know if that's a good idea for tonight Mya. You really should be resting. You've been at school all week, doing a lot of moving around. I need you to take it easy. Going to the mall may not be good." Mom replied.

"Come on Mom, I'll rest for an hour. Then can we go, please? I really need some new clothes." I said.

"Mya..ask your dad. I really don't know." Mom said.

"Mom, how about tomorrow then? I'll rest all day." I said.

"That sounds better, we can go in the morning after breakfast." Mom said.

"Now, go upstairs and rest please baby girl," Mom added.

"I will mom," I replied.
I really wish that my parents would just let go a little. I feel like I'm still a baby in this house. When I go to school, I finally feel free. I feel like a teenager. Not a normal teenager, but a teenager. I love my parents. But ugh. They will never let go. All I really wanted to do today was school, shop, then go to bed. That plan failed.

So, I go back upstairs, gets in bed, and brings my computer out. As I was searching for a movie to watch on Netflix, I just decided to write in my diary instead.

I haven't written anything in my diary in such a long time. I usually write in my journal when something really good happens, or something really bad happens.

Mya's Diary Entry:

Dear Diary,

I have neglected my diary for a while, but I'm back. There wasn't much happening in my life for a while, until school started. Within a couple weeks, my life went from zero to one hundred. It just changed so fast.

Certain things will never change, you know the usual things. Mom and dad are still very over protective of me and never want me to grow up.

They don't trust that I will be okay. Cerebral palsy is still living inside of me, and I am still struggling from day to day. Starting school was nerve wrecking, and very rough. But it wasn't all bad. Don't worry diary.

When I first got there the halls were so crowded and kids were running to class. I almost got ran over. I was lost and didn't know where to go, but this nice man escorted me to class.

The nice man is my new guidance counselor at Springville. He's awesome. Too bad I won't see him next year because I'll be moving to the high school. Wow, I haven't really thought about that. Me, being a freshman in high school. Sounds pretty terrifying. But anyway, back to the update. I became friends with two pretty cool people at school, Steven and Corrine. I still have a lot to learn about them, of course. But they are nice. They've even hung out at my house twice.

I guess I should mention how a group of girls followed me to the bathroom, knocked me down, and threw my walker down to the ground. They were also chanting a bunch of mean things. Why do people always pick on crippled people? I mean really, we deal with enough. I hate bullies. Seriously, it really sucked. Of course, mom and dad freaked out and wanted to take me out of school. I said no way. I guess that's something positive for your diary. I have developed serious tough skin and guts. I'm even starting my own club at school called, The Unpretty Project for girls. You of all people know how many times I've felt unpretty. It's not fun, and the bullies at Springville don't help.

Well, that's pretty much the gist of what's been going on with me. My health is fine, I think. Lately, I haven't felt the best but it comes with having Cerebral Palsy. It happens. I need to remember that although I'm trying to be a normal student, that will never really happen. I can only be Mya Iverson, and Mya Iverson is far from normal. I don't know if people will love me for me, but only time will tell diary. You've always been my best friend. Writing is my safe space. I will try to give you constant updates, throughout my new life. Yes, new. This is all so new to me. I'm living in a different world.

The next day,

"Mya! Mya! Wake up, honey. Time for shopping. You still want to go, don't you?" Mom said in a cheerful voice.

"ugh," I moaned and grunted.

"You did all that whining yesterday, you better get up girl. I'm ready." Mom said.

"Can't I sleep for like twenty more minutes? Why so early? It's only ten in the morning mom. Really? I haven't really been able to sleep in since school started!" I whined to my mom.

"You have ten minutes to get dressed Mya, I have to work tonight." Mom said.

"Alright mom, I'm up, I'm up. Seriously." I grunted again. I was so sleepy.

I finally get up to get dressed, even though I feel so exhausted this morning. I head downstairs and my mom is already waiting for me at the door.

"Mom, really? You weren't playing I see." I said sarcastically.

"Quit the attitude. You'll live. It's not that early girlfriend." Mom said.

"If you say so", I shrugged.

Mom and I get in the car and head to the mall. I am super annoyed at mom for waking me up so early. I was hoping that we would go later in the day or at night. I was really looking forward to sleeping in and enjoying my comfy bed. She should know that I really haven't had an easy time with getting sleep lately.

I've been worrying about school every night and planning my days in my head. I'm going to attempt to shake this off and be grateful that we are spending time together. Finally, I'm getting some new clothes to sport at school, so I won't be totally lame.

When my mom and I arrive at the mall, she asked what stores I'd want to check out. Honestly, I have no idea. Shopping isn't my thing. But I've heard of a few stores that teenagers usually shop in like forever 21, garage, and charlotte russe. I've never stepped foot into any of those stores, but I hear they are very popular. The only stores I really go in are grocery and department stores. Sadly. I'm like an old lady. My mom takes me to old navy a lot though. I like them. I think I want to try out forever 21. I looked at some of their tops on their website and actually liked them. Who knows, I may find a couple outfits that will look nice on me. I know mom is going to freak out when we start shopping. She lives for this stuff. Seriously. Lord help me. I hope that I don't get a headache. Gotta love mom though. I feel like I should have been a boy. Life would be so much easier.

"Mya, where do you want to go love?" Mom said as she looks ready to shop. She even wore sneakers, she means business. Ha-ha.

"Mom, I'm not quite sure. We can try forever 21. I've heard a lot about it and saw a few things online that I'd like. Let's go there." I said.

"Okay sure. I've walked past it a few times, it's on the first floor. Let's hit it!" Mom said with excitement.

Mom and I walk to forever 21 passing several stores that I know nothing about. I kinda want to start coming to the mall, especially now that I have friends. Maybe Steven and Corrine will want to hang out at the mall sometime. I texted both of them actually and started a group chat. This is so cool. Me? Being in a group chat with friends. It's so unreal.

"Oo Mya, you have to try a couple of these fall sweaters that they have on sale! They are so cute. You could wear them with cute jeans with boots." Mom said, way too happily.
I actually agreed with my mom. She has good taste in clothes, and she is super stylish. I'm going to try on the sweaters. Hopefully try some jeans on too.

"Mom, I like these. I was thinking of getting a pair of those ugg boots too. If that's okay." I asked.

"Of course. I wanted to buy these for you before but you said no." Mom said.

"Well, yeah. I want to change up a little bit now." I said.

"I'm going to try on some jeans too mom," I added.

My mom nodded her head.
So, I go in the fitting room to try on the sweaters and jeans. I love it all. This is so cool. Shopping. I never would've thought I'd like shopping. Maybe it's just because I haven't had new clothes in so long. It feels good.

"Hey mom, I want three of these sweaters and three pairs of jeans that I tried on. Is that okay? Then maybe some boots and sneakers?" I said.

"Yeah, it's fine. I don't mind spending money. You never ever ask for anything. It's my pleasure. I love treating you, and I'm happy to be spending some quality time with my daughter." Mom said.

So, forever 21 was a good pick. They had more stuff that I actually liked. I'll probably ask to go back eventually. I just wanted a couple of new things for now. I guess retail therapy is a real thing. Who knew? Now, mom and I are going to buy the boots and sneakers for me to wear. My feet have been looking pretty bad. Steven and Corrine will probably be super shocked to see me in new clothes on Monday. It will be obvious that my clothes are new, they look totally different from what I've been wearing.

"Thank you, mom, for taking the time out today and shopping with me!" I said while smiling.

"You are more than welcome Mya. Let me know when you want to go shopping for some more things. Maybe next month or in a few weeks we can get you some more tops." Mom said.

"You're the best mom. Now can we go home and eat, I'm starved." I asked.

"We are heading there now, as soon as I get your walker back into the car." Mom said.

"I've been using my walker a lot more these days. I think all the walking at school is having an impact on my muscles or bones. It's best I use it, no matter if kids laugh or stare." I said as she looked out of the window.

"Now you know not to talk like that around me, I'm already nervous enough about this school thing. But I'm proud of you for sticking through. Most kids would've quit by now. But not you, not my baby. You are pushing through every single day, and I know it isn't easy. Sometimes I wish that I could take all of your pain away, and insecurities." Mom said.

"Thanks, mom. You can always uplift me when I'm feeling unpretty. I want to help other kids like me, and other girls who feel unpretty. You and dad don't have to worry about me." I said as me and mom are cheesing at each other with love.

Chapter 7

The magic in me, maybe grandma was onto something

Monday Morning,

Well, the weekend is over and I am starting my day at school. I get to my first-period class and the teacher announces that we are having an assembly today. This is a surprise assembly! I knew nothing about this. None of us did. I'm not complaining though, maybe it'll be interesting.

But I am worried about who I will be sitting with. I'm going to check my group chat and try to catch up with Steven and Corrine. Steven and Corrine are on their way to the assembly and so am I. I'll be keeping my eyes wide open so that I can spot them.

"Mya!" someone yelled across the hall. It sounds like Corrine. She doesn't really talk much, so her voice is hard to make out. I'm pretty sure it's her though because that is not Steven's voice and nobody else knows my name. Just the truth. The voice gets closer and I can finally see her. Now we need to find Steven.

"Steven, Steven!" I yelled, in hopes of him just hearing my yells.

I tried to yell for Steven, but no answer. My phone vibrates and it is a text from Steven. The text read, "Hey guys, I'm already in the auditorium, towards the left side in the back." I didn't really want to sit in the back, but I guess that'll do. Corrine and I catch up with Steven, he saved two seats for us.

"Hey, guys!" Steven said.

"Hey, Steven!" Corrine and I both said.

"So, does anyone know what this assembly is about? They said we will be starting as soon as all of the classes in the eighth grade are present." Steven said.

"Nope," Corrine replied.

"No idea," I replied.

The lights all of a sudden begin to dim in the auditorium. I guess the assembly is about to begin. My first time sitting in a school assembly. A projector screen pops up and the first thing I see a photo of a kid on the back of a school bus being bullied. In the picture, kids are throwing paper balls at him and he is covering his face with his book bag. So, this assembly is about bullying? Very interesting. A major coincidence. I was thrown to the ground by girls at Springville, and now all of a sudden, we are having an assembly about bullying.

I really don't know how I feel about this because the entire school heard about what happened to me. It's kinda embarrassing. I feel like everyone is going to be looking at me, and talking about me after it is over. I wish I would've stayed home today like mom and dad wanted me to. For now, I'll try to remain positive.

"Mya, are you good?" Corrine asked in a nervous voice.

"Yeah, I'm good. I just think that this is a huge coincidence. Don't you? It's a little strange. I feel put on the spot but this wouldn't be the first time. So, to answer your question, yes, I'm good. It's whatever." I replied to Corrine probably sounding extremely aggravated.

So, a speaker comes up and says, "Welcome to our No bullies allowed program, where bullies are allowed. Very catchy huh? Well, we want bullies here so that they can be convinced to stop for a number of reasons."

That was catchy, I give him that. Then he has people handing out little pamphlets with all kinds of bullying statistics, and hotline numbers to call for depressed or suicidal thoughts. Despite, my thoughts about how this assembly came about, this is pretty cool. It reminds me of some ideas that I have for The Unpretty Project. I hate bullies and what they do. They make people feel so low, and that's how I felt when my face was smashed against the floor while my walker was flipped over. I felt low, or Unpretty.

I see Mr. Davids standing up there with the main speaker. I should've known he was behind this. He probably thought I'd like this idea, and I do. But I wish it was later in the year. Not within the same month, I was the talk of the school. But hey, what can I do? It's happening and people are definitely looking back at me laughing. I even heard someone say, "That Iverson girl." It starts now, I guess.

"You guys, this is extremely boring. Don't get me wrong, this is important but God. This is boring. I want to sleep now." Steven said as his head kept nodding off during the assembly presentation.

"Oh Steven, stop complaining. At least people are laughing and staring at you." I said while rolling my eyes at Steven.

"She's got a point there Steven, they are starring," Corrine said.

"It shouldn't be too long though. They don't like to keep us out of class too long Mya." Steven said.

"True, shouldn't be much longer My," Corrine said.

I guess Corrine gave me a nickname, "My". My dad calls me that all the time. This is a new level of friendship maybe. Giving out nicknames! I said.

"I wanna call you that too. Corrine isn't the only one who can call you by a nickname." Steven said.

"Ha-ha, guys call me whatever. Seriously. I'll have to think of nicknames for you both." I said.

So, the assembly is coming to a conclusion, and they end with asking if anyone has questions. And of course, a few hands went up which made me extremely nervous. One girl said, "how do you know someone is telling the truth about being bullied, cause you know sometimes people just want attention."

Then a few people around her started yelling and agreeing with her. Some teenagers can be so obnoxious, I guess we see who the bullies are now. Although those were not the particular girls who bullied me. They're probably friends though. Snotty, wannabe tough girls. I'm the tough one, as my mom would say.

Then someone else said, "Well, how will you catch the bullies?" Everyone turned and looked at her. I've never seen this girl before. Maybe she's been bullied before, or maybe she's just curious. I actually am too. What would really happen to these bullies? There should be a consequence more than just a day out of school. They probably enjoy those suspended days off.

Right when someone was about to ask another question, a kid yelled, "Mya what do you think?" I just decided to ignore that comment. How do you bully someone during a bullying assembly? Sad. But surprisingly, I don't care. I'm content, and just fine. Spending time with my mom this past weekend, and having my new friends put me in such a good space. It definitely sucks that people are such jerks, but maybe this is just a fact of life. Eighth grade is hard, but thankfully I was able to start in eighth grade instead of the high school. That would've been a complete nightmare. Probably would rather just stay home at that point. I still wish mom and let would've let me start school sooner, eighth grade is still pretty late in the game.

The assembly is over and everyone is walking back to their classes. Steven, Corrine and I go our separate ways since we all have different classes. It would be so cool having them in some of my classes. I'm a total outcast in my classes. My phone vibrates again and it's my dad texting me. The text reads, "Let me know if you want us to pick you up, heard about assembly." Oh gosh, when will it end. I wonder if anyone else's parents are like this or are mine just crazy. Could be because I'm their kid, besides our dog. He's a part of the family too!

As I'm walking to class, I hear a voice.

"Hey Ms. Iverson, how did you like the assembly?" It was Mr. Davids, of course.

"It was good, the timing was a little strange but good," I replied starring Mr. Davids right into his eyes.

"Oh Mya, this was actually scheduled since the summer time. We've been having some serious bullying issues at Springville out of nowhere. It wasn't always like this, so we need to get down to the bottom of this. That's why we scheduled the assembly." Mr. Davids said.

"Oh," I replied, feeling stupid.

"Yes, so hopefully people got the message so what happened to you will never happen again." Mr. Davids said with hope.

"hopefully," I replied.

I feel like a jerk for assuming that he planned that assembly solely because of me. It definitely was awkward since everyone knew what happened, but I shouldn't have assumed.

After school that day

It's time for my meeting, my very first meeting and I'm super excited. I can't believe I actually started something, with the help of my two friends and guidance counselor of course. This is great. You know what? I was so concerned with people not coming out but even if five people come, I'm satisfied. For now, at least. My friends and I are in the cafeteria, setting up. After I told mom about this, she offered to bring refreshments. So, it's looking pretty good. So far nobody is here besides myself, two friends and Mr. Davids.

The four of us start to eat the refreshments thinking they we may have to try again on another day, until we saw three girls come into the cafeteria and sit down. Then two more girls came in ten minutes later. The last two girls are both disabled. One is using a crutch and the other one is in a wheelchair. This is exactly what I wanted to happen.

At the meeting, we exchanged cell phone numbers and created a group chat for The Unpretty Project. We also picked a date to collect donations for our winter clothing drive. The meeting was cool, especially for the first one. I knew a lot of people wouldn't come, but some did. That made me extremely happy. Mr. Davids was so proud of me, for taking a chance. The new girl who uses a walker and has cerebral palsy creating a school club to help others. I'm actually proud of myself. Definitely not feeling Unpretty. Ha-Ha. I can't wait to go home and tell my parents all about it. I plan to get to know all the people who came out personally. Springville doesn't seem too bad after all.

After the meeting, I had to walk to my classroom to get some of my belongings that I left behind before going to the meeting. When I go into the classroom it is empty. I wonder where my teacher is. I grabbed my things and headed towards the door. As I walked out of the door, I ran into the same group of girls who bullied me when I first got to Springville. Literally ran into them.

"Well, if it isn't Ms. Tattle tale snitch." One of them said.

"Get out of my way!" I said.

"Or what, you'll call Mr. Davids? Where is he now? Never around when you need him huh? He's only good for lecturing us about stupid stuff, that you lie about." She said.

"Lie?" I questioned.

"Yes, lie. You said that we pushed you to the ground and knocked over your stupid little handicapped walker. That's a lie, you fell because you were scared of us." She said, while her crew just stared.

To my surprise, the others with her aren't really saying much. Maybe deep down they know that she is wrong for treating me this way but peer pressure is a real thing.

"You pushed me down and you know it. Move. I need to get home." I yelled at the top of my lungs.

She stood in front of me, and I started to get so angry that something weird began to happen. I began to feel really weird. I'm not sure how what's going on but it's not cerebral palsy related. This is different, very different. The girl starts to move back away from me. She starts to chant, "Mya the freak, Mya the freak."

Before I knew it, she flew across the hall and her friends ran in fear. I'm not so sure what happened. All I know is that I looked at her with anger and the next second she was flying across the hall. I am filled up with confusion and just want to go home. It was almost as if magic did it, or some serious wind. I don't know.

Mom is outside waiting for me to come get into the car so that we can go inside. I don't even know how I'm going to talk to her with what just happened on my mind. I get into the car and mom is already asking questions.

"Hey honey, how was the meeting? Give me all the details and don't leave anything out!" My mom said.

I paused before I answered and took a deep breath. Finally, I responded and said, "Hi mom, umm it was great. A decent amount of people came out, and we all had a good time."

"So, what about your clothing drive for charity? Is that a go?" Mom asked.

"Yup it is," I answered barely paying attention to my mother.

"Are you okay? Are you sure everything went alright? It sounds like it did but you're acting funny." Mom wondered.

"Yes, just exhausted. Long day mom." I answered.

"Understandable. You look nice in your new clothes Mya," Mom said.

"Thanks, mommy." I replied.

So, I get home and immediately go upstairs to my room. I didn't even find my dad to say hello. I'm just so lost for words. I think that I may be magic. As crazy as it sounds. If I am magic, I'm super freaked that all of those mean kids saw. They will tell everyone about what happened, but people probably wouldn't believe them.

 I get on google, to try to make sense of it all. Google has all the answers, right? Well, so far, I see all these weird sites about magical stuff that I'm not even into. This just makes me think about how my grandmother always said there was something different about me, beyond cerebral palsy. She knew something. Or maybe she was magic. Stop it Mya! You're not magic.

Google says that what happened, is describing telekinesis. Could it be so? No way. I'm the crippled girl. But what else could explain what happened? Nothing. I'm going to try to get it to happen again. If I could move her, maybe I can move an object.

I went downstairs to the basement where there is a lot of space to try to figure this thing out. So, what should I try to move or fly across the room? I'm not sure..maybe that old vase. I'm sure mom won't miss it. That thing has been down here for years. If she wanted it, she would have it set up for people to see.

So, the internet says telekinesis works when you are really focused on an object. I was staring really hard at that girl with anger right before she flew. I'm going to stare at this vase and see what happens.

I stood up and looked directly at the vase and stared. But nothing happens.

I must be a fool for trying this. But to think, whatever did happen I'm glad it did. Because when I think about how mean that girl was being I could SCREAM!

As I said those words, the vase flew across the room and smashed into the wall. The vase created a massive hole in the wall. "WHOA BABY," I screamed, covering her mouth really fast so that her parents wouldn't hear her.

I figured it out! It works when I'm thinking about something or someone that angers me or makes me upset.

Mya Iverson, the thirteen-year-old girl who has cerebral palsy and superpowers. This year just keeps getting weirder and weirder. I'm not sure if this new-found power is a good or bad thing. But, it will be my little secret. I don't even want to write about this in my diary.

Chapter 8

Me, myself, and my magic

I asked my parents if I could stay home from school today, and of course, they said yes. They miss me being home during the day. The house must be different without me. Plus, just last week they were begging me to stay home out of fear. I told them that I wasn't feeling well and that I was too weak to walk. I mean, that's not all the way false.

I actually don't feel well, but I usually just push through the pain. I just can't go back to school right now after finding out that I can literally move things with my mind. I want to practice it and get better. The next time those bullies mess with anyone, I'll use them again. It'll scare the crap out of them. I do think that they will try to tell everyone, but it may end up making them look like the crazy ones. But, for now, I'll be home for the day.

I received text messages from both group chats that I have now. One with Steven and Corrine, then the other one with the new members of the group that I started. Everyone is wondering where I am, and if I was okay. I guess because nobody saw me after the meeting ended. I want to tell Steven and Corrine about this superpower, but they may be totally freaked out. I wouldn't blame them though. I'm totally freaked out myself.

I'm going to respond to both group chats and say, "Thanks for checking up on me, cerebral palsy had its way today. Not feeling well."

I know that's not the complete truth, but I had to say something. Hopefully, they leave it at that, and don't ask me anything else. I would hate to keep lying or not being truthful, but this secret has to stay a secret. I really want to practice using this magical power, however, that'll be impossible without my mom or dad catching me. Maybe one day I'll tell them since they're my parents, not now though. They will be so confused, but who knows, maybe mom or dad have a magical power. I'm not sure if this stuff is inherited. Or maybe grandma had magical powers.

"Mya, are you hungry? Your mom is making breakfast! Pancakes, eggs, and bacon. Yum!" Dad said.

"Umm, honestly not really dad. I just want to rest."

"Well, its downstairs honey." Dad insisted.

"Alright dad thanks, can you please close the door," I asked.

My dad closed the door, and I was feeling so overwhelmed that I decided to take a nap.

A few hours later.

"Mya! Wake up, Mya." Mom yelled up the stairs.

I grunted and moaned in bed.

"Mya your friends are here to see you." Mom said.

I immediately grabbed my phone to see if I missed any text messages, which I did. Both of my new group chats were going off repeatedly while I was asleep. I get up out of bed, get dressed, grabbed my walker and go downstairs to greet my friends.

"Hi, guys. What a surprise." I said sarcastically.

"What's up homie!" Steven said, as the others went up to me and hugged me.

"We just wanted to come by since you were feeling well." Corrine said.

"Well, you guys definitely surprised me. Thanks." I replied.

I want to be happy they are there, but I am still concerned that my superpower may come out. I don't know how to control it yet.

"I have snacks for you guys, but then Mya needs to rest to be energized for school." Mom said.

My friends grab all the snacks and head to the basement.

"So, what's up Mya, are you feeling better?" Steven asked.

"Yes, just tired. I'm happy you guys came through. That was very thoughtful." I said.

"So, are you guys ready to collect donations this week?" Corrine asked.

"Oh yes. Yeah." Everyone replied.

"My grandmother has a box of hats and gloves that she would like to donate, I'll just bring it to school when we start to collect." One of the new girls from the group said.

"Awesome, anyone else bringing clothing donations from home?" I asked.

"This may sound like a dumb question, but do the clothing have to be for girls?" Steven asked.

"Of course not, you should know that Steven," I answered.

"Okay, cause I have a ton of things I can donate," Steven said.

"Well let's keep in mind that we don't want to be donating anything that isn't new or barely used. Nobody wants old, raggedy clothes. Even the homeless people deserve better." I said.

"So, what are you trying to say friend, you gotta give me more credit than that. I would never just give away junk." Steven yelled."

"Just putting it out their buddy." I answered.

I get up and go to get something to drink. While I am upstairs, I asked my mom to go downstairs and say that it is time for me to rest again. I told my mom that I wasn't feeling well, but didn't want to just kick them out. It would be easier if my mom just asked them politely. And she agreed, thank God.

Little does my mom know...I am not having a cerebral palsy problem. More like, a magical problem going on.

"Mya needs to rest everyone, but feel free to visit her anytime. Her dad and I appreciate you thinking of her. It means so much. But right now, she needs to take it easy." Mom said.

"See you in school guys. Be ready to set up our donation table and collect hats and gloves. Mr. Davids put flyers all around the building, so people should be aware." I said.

"We got you Mya," Steven said and winked at me.

Everyone told me to feel better and left to go home. I went straight upstairs to my room, and my mother followed me. Of course.

"Mom, really though," I whispered underneath my breath.

"Yes, really. You don't feel good, I want to help you." Mom said.

"But I can walk alone, I can go to my room without you following me." I replied.

"Girl, who are you talking to? Must be somebody else in the room." Mom said in her stern voice.

I turned my head away from my mom and rolled my eyes as my mom still continues to follow me to my room.

"I saw that." Mom said.

"Saw what exactly?" I asked.

"I used to roll my eyes at your grandmother all the time, so I know that's exactly what you just did. Just know I know girlfriend. Now get in your bed, and I'll close the door." Mom said.

Finally, I get to be alone in my room. This magic thing is seriously on my mind. It's going to take a long time for me to adjust, or even understand this. What are they for? Maybe protection? I wish someone else had superpowers that I knew. I thought this stuff only existed in the movies, boy was I wrong. There are probably thousands of others in this world with magical powers.

There is no way possible that I am the only one on this planet with magic living inside of me. The more I think about it, this may be a good thing. I'll never be pushed to the ground again.

I am curious to see how those girls will react when they see me in school tomorrow. Ha-ha, maybe they stayed home for a day too. They're probably traumatized. Good for them. Is that a mean thing to say? Well, I meant it. That girl and her little posse deserved to be scared for once. They are always scaring everyone else. All the time. What goes around comes around.

Now, I need to figure out how to hide my power. Not like I know how to use it anyway, but I don't want things in class just randomly moving and flying across the room because I'm looking at it. Especially since sometimes I stare into space or at an object when class gets really boring. I can't help it. I think it only works when I'm angry or frustrated though. I need to figure this all out. Maybe go to google again. Google has all the answers.

I think, for now, I just have to be really careful. I will just be praying and hoping that the magical me won't show. This is my secret, although I really want to tell Steven and Corrine. I probably shouldn't. At least for now.

The Next Day

"Good Morning Mya!" Mom said

"Good Morning Mom," I replied.

"Let me know when you're ready to leave for school. I'll be downstairs eating my fruit for breakfast." Mom said.

"Okay, be down in a minute mommy," I replied.

So today I am wearing another new outfit, and confidence will be my style. I realized that no matter what I'm going to be different. Especially now. This is beyond being different. I am magical. I have a gift. I guess this is a blessing? Still haven't figured that out yet. But right now, I'm loving it. Yet, still somewhat freaked out.

When I see those girls, I will be smiling. Well, I shouldn't look at them too hard. Maybe cause a human tornado, if you know what I mean. I don't think that they've told anyone yet because Steven and Corrine would have heard something and texted me. Nothing yet, so that's good. My gut tells me that eventually, they will though. They would not give up an opportunity to totally embarrass me. But, they can bring it on. I'm ready for any challenge.

My life has been very peculiar lately. I think that it is for the good. I always think back to how boring life was, compared to know. Now I am a student, a friend, president of a school club, and I have magic in me. Literally magic. I haven't even been thinking about my condition. Mom and dad don't think that's good though. They are probably right, but for once cerebral palsy isn't my entire life. I know that my health needs to come first, but who knows. Maybe this new-found gift will completely cure me of my condition. How can I be magic and still be sick? It doesn't make much sense to me. But as of right now, cerebral palsy is still in me. I know because my bones and body hurt, I still need a walker, and my speech hasn't been all the way normal.

I went downstairs, ate a little cereal and fruit for breakfast before leaving for school. My mom is staring at me like she knows something is up. She probably does. Mothers always know. I guess that's a gift too.

"Mya, you're glowing this morning." Mom said.

"Glowing? What does that even mean?" I asked sarcastically.

"It means that you are glowing. You look happier than usual this morning. I wonder what's going on with you. Must be something." Mom said.

"Nothing is going on...can't a girl look happy?" I said.

"Alrighty. If you say so, Mya. But just know that I'm on to you. Must be a boy involved or something. I'm watching you." Mom said while giggling and making kissy faces at me.

"Oh God mom, please. Spare me. I'm not even thinking about boys." I said.

"Well, there's Steven." Mom said.

"Ummm, he's a friend. No more, no less." I replied.

"If you say so." Mom said.

Me and my mom ride in silence for the rest of the way to school, up until my arrival.

"Bye, mom." I said.

"Bye Ms. Glowing. I love you," Mom said.

"I love you too," I replied, after exiting the car.

I'm back at Springville, ready to begin the day. I need to get all of the homework and notes that I missed from yesterday. Keeping up with my grades should be a priority on my list. Not that I'm really concerned, but I know mom is going to ask where is my homework. She is definitely going to bug me about having my head in the books. I don't want her to say that my new friends, or group are distracting me from doing my best in all of my classes. I'll make tonight, a study night. A study night for school work and magic. Busy is going to soon be my middle name. But this is what I wanted.

Usually, I see Steven early in the morning, but he must be in class already. I was actually going to ask him for help. I'm feeling a little weak. I was seriously hoping that the magic powers would do some abracadabra on my body. That would be better than being able to move things with my mind.

I went to my first-period class where nobody speaks to her. I sat in the front row hoping that the day will go by super-fast.

"Good Morning class! Today will be a unique class. I will not be standing up front teaching the usual traditionally style. We will have stations, and you guys will do the different assignments in each station in groups. Each group will have only ten minutes to answer the question in your station. You should bring your notes out and communicate with each other." The teacher said.

Now I am completely annoyed already. I cringe at the thought of being forced to work in groups. Shouldn't this be an option? I guess not. It's weird how I am making some progress with socializing, but not really in the classroom. Oh well. I'm going to just try to get through this little activity to get it over with.

"Hey everyone. We have ten minutes so let's get started." One of my classmates said.

"Agreed," I replied.

We completed the work, without hardly any social interaction. These kids think that I'm going to bite them or something, or that I'm contagious. It's really starting to get annoying. What makes them think they are better than me? Or what makes them think that I'm not good enough to be their friend, or even good enough to talk to. I guess this walker, and my condition scares them. People tend to fear what they don't understand.

Later that day, I went to the cafeteria to prepare to eat lunch and collect donations with my new team. I have three big boxes prepared for all the donations, so hopefully, I get a good amount of clothing.

"Hey Mya, I have my donations ready. Where do I put them?" A random girl said.

"You're the very first donation! The box is right here, I decorated it myself. Do you like it?" I replied.

"It's cute! Well, here ya go. I had all these things in my closet at home." The random girl replied.

After the first donation, a large line formed of several teachers.

"Hey Mya, looks like this is a success so far," Steven said.

Corrine is entering the café late. But she rushed over to Steven and me to give her donations.

"Hey guys, sorry I'm late but here are my donations," Corrine said.

"Hey girl, here is the box. Drop your stuff in." I said.

"Wow, all these teachers are supporting," Steven said.

"Yeah, it looks like all of the donations are coming from teachers…" I said in a sad tone.

"Donations are donations. Who cares where they come from?" Steven said, in hopes of making me happy.

"Stevens right!" Corrine said.

"I guess so. It's just a shame how students won't give to a good cause because of whose running it, the crippled girl." I said.

"The kick-butt tough crippled girl!" Steven said while hugging me.

Corrine, Steven and I start laughing, and continue to collect donations during lunch time. Most of the donations came from teachers, and just a few students. When Lunch is over, Mr. Davids along with two other staff members come over to grab all the donations and store them away.

At the end of the day, I realized that I had collected over one hundred hats, fifty pairs of gloves, and fifty different scarves.

"I'll text you tonight," Steven said as he was leaving the school building.

"Okay," I answered.

I am happy about all the donations, but I have to be completely honest and admit that students, not donating a lot is very disappointing to me. I guess it is what it is. But Jeeze. Am I that weird or strange that you can even support my charity function? I guess in their small minds it's like a charity case trying to help other charity cases.

Well, Mya Iverson may be a lot of things but one thing I am not is a charity case. I just have to deal with a condition that is out of my control, but that does not make me a charity case. Maybe I should just come to terms with the fact that some people will never see passed cerebral palsy.

So You Think You're Unpretty?

Chapter 9

Shall I dance with a walker by my side

Today begins another school day, and I am super tired. More like exhausted. I'm ready for it to be over already. I guess mom was right about me paying more attention to my health. I've been neglecting my health responsibilities and now I can see the results of that. I'll be sure to take my medicine, vitamins, do my exercises and see my nurse over the weekend. Moms are always right. I'm totally convinced of that. My muscles are feeling really tight, and I think that I'm about to start having muscle spasms in my leg. My mom usually is always right, as much as I hate to admit that. Because today, Is just physically not my day. So much for being magical. What's the use, if I can cure myself.

As I walk through the halls ways, I notice an interesting flyer on the wall. The flyer is apparently for a fall homecoming dance. I thought that was only for high school. I guess this is more like a junior homecoming? Who knows. Should I even consider going? I don't really dance, but it may be fun. The food may be good, and I know like two or three dances.

I wonder if Steven and Corrine knew about this dance. They haven't mentioned anything to me about it, but they had to know about it. They've been students their whole lives. I'm sure they are aware of all the dances and school activities. They probably figured that I wouldn't want to go because I usually use my walker to walk. But, so what. I can bring it or not bring it to the dance, that's if I decide to go.

The dance is at the end of this week! How did I not know about this? It's almost as if everyone was trying to keep it from me. Mr. Davids didn't even mention it to me. The flyer says that it is Friday, and begins at seven. Also, you have to pay to get inside, but I don't mind that. Surprisingly I would like to go.

I grabbed the flyer and walk away continuing to look at it. As I began to walk those bullies start walking towards me out of nowhere making mean comments. I've got to stop running into them.

"Keep walking!" I said.

"Well, somebody's got some confidence now huh?" somebody said, but I could not see who. So, I kept walking straight, trying to avoid them.

"You're a freak! We know you have a secret! We are going to tell everyone that you're some kind of magical freak, or witch." Somebody from the group yelled.

I continued to walk forward using my walker, and I began to shed many tears. My face started to turn red, and I felt herself getting extremely angry.

"Stay calm, Stay calm," I repeated to myself over and over again trying to refrain from getting too angry. I don't want to get so upset that I end up using my magical power again. This time could cause major exposure.

"Get angry. Use your powers freak. How does someone with magic, still use a walker? It's probably a cover-up. She probably walks perfectly fine. She just doesn't want to be exposed." A boy in the group of bullies yelled.

"Leave me alone! For the last, and very last time." I cried.

I began to cry and scream, "Help, Help" as they kept following me down the hall. A teacher ran out and said, "Leave her alone!" All of the bullies ran quickly down the hall. They disappeared.
"

Are you alright?" The teacher asked me.

"No, I am not. I want to go home! Now!" I demanded.

The teacher walked me to the front office and called my mother. My mother immediately hung the phone up and headed to the school to see about me. When she arrived to the school, my mom put me in the car and took me home. The car ride was completely silent because I really did not want to speak at the moment. I was totally way too fed up. After everything, they still hadn't learned anything or changed their behavior.

When I got home, I went to my room and began to throw and kick things all around. All of a sudden, I began to move objects around in my room with my mind. It was so amazing. Things were floating in the air and flying. In that moment, I felt powerful.

Knock Knock! Mom knocked on the door.

"Don't come in mom, please. I need a little time to myself." I replied.

"Time to yourself? In my house?" Mom said.

"Honey, give her an hour or so to just chill," Dad whispered to mom loudly.

"You have one hour and then I'm coming in to speak with you." Mom said then left me to herself.

I cannot believe today. I just cannot. I can't keep missing school because of these bullies. I guess that assembly didn't help at all. Instead, it made matters worse. I guess me using my magical powers and flying that girl in the air to get her away from me wasn't enough. They just will not stop messing with me. They refuse. I'm sure that there has to be others. Other victims of their bullying.

On another note, my power seems to be stronger. It's either stronger or I'm just understanding how it works now. When I fully get the handle of this, I will show those bullies. I won't try to hurt them, just give a good scare. Obviously, the last time didn't do much.

They said that they were going to start telling people about what they saw. I am not quite sure what I'd say to other kids in school when they ask. I will deny of course. But hopefully, I'm not a bad liar. My family always says that I'm a bad liar, so usually, honesty is my best policy.

I just received text messages from Steven and Corrine. Steven said, "Yo, Mya, where are you?"

Part of me really wants to just ignore the messages that they send since they didn't tell me about the dance. Yes, the dance is still on my mind. I have never been to anything like this before, and it would've been nice if they at least mentioned it. Maybe I'll bring it up now.

"I'm home. I had an emergency but everything is just fine. Thanks." I said.

"Okay well, are you going to be in school tomorrow?" Corrine and Steven both asked.

"Yes, I will. But I have a question for you guys." I said.
"Uhm, alright. Go for it." Steven said.

"Did you guys know about the upcoming homecoming dance?" I asked.

Nobody responded in their group chat for over an over, until finally, Steven said something back.

Steven replied, "Well, yeah we knew about it. It's really not a big deal. Just a dance."

Corrine still hasn't said anything back, but I responded to Steven.

"Why wouldn't you guys tell me? I really would've liked to have known. School is new to me remember? Did you guys plan to go without me?" I asked.

"Nope. I wasn't going to go at all. I'm a nobody. Why would I be going to a homecoming dance with kids who don't ever acknowledge my existence?" Steven said.

"Well, you know what. I think we should go! We could even invite the few people who came to my first meeting at school." I said.

"Mya that would be fine. But there's one problem." Steven said.

"What's that?" I asked.

"People usually have dates at these types of events. We would look totally lame." Steven said.

"Couldn't we be like friend dates then?" I insisted because I really want to go.

"I don't see why not." Steven happily answered with a smiley face emoji.

"Well then, it's a date, my friend," I said.

"I guess it is," Steven said.

"Wait, does this mean I have to pay for both tickets? Ha-Ha, I'm kind of broke." Steven jokingly said.

"No way. I have mine covered. I got it." I assured Steven.

"Okay cool, then it's definitely a date," Steven said.

I am so excited to go to this dance. My very first dance ever. I just need to make sure I control my power. I can feel it growing inside of me, which can be good or bad. Getting exposed can never be an option. My life would be over. I wonder If I'd go to jail or be locked away? People are always afraid of real magic, or anything that they don't understand. I mean, I'd be scared too. This is a bizarre thing to get used to. I don't know when I'll ever get used to being able to move things with my mind. But for right now, this dance is my focus. I can't wait to tell my mom.

I yelled to my mom for her to come upstairs so that I can share the news.

"Mom! Mom!" I kept yelling to get her attention.

My mom runs up the stairs and goes into my room so fast.

"Yes! What it is, what's wrong?" Mom asked.

"I have good news for you. You're going to be super excited!" I said.

"Okay, spill the beans! Don't beat around the bush please, you know that I hate surprises." Mom said in her impatient voice.

"Alright well here it goes, you're not even going to believe this," I said.

"Spill it!" Mom yelled, and shook me! Mom can be impatient.

"I'm going to the fall homecoming dance! I said in a loud, cheerful voice.

"What!! You're kidding." Mom said.

"Nope, I'm dead serious. And wait, there's more!" I said.

"More? What more?" Mom said.

"Steven and I are going to go together as dates. Well, not a boyfriend, girlfriend type of date. More like friends going on a date together." I said with a smirk on my face.

"Oh, wait until I tell your father! I guess we will be going shopping again! This is the best news that I've heard in a while. I'm so happy that you are spreading your wings, my love." Mom said.

"Yeah, it's pretty exciting. I can't wait to go. I won't be dancing, but just dressing up will be fun." I said.

"Of course, it will! I'll be right there to help." Mom said.

Mom left to go tell dad about the homecoming dance! She is almost just as excited as me. She can't wait to help me pick out a dress and get ready. She'll probably end up taking a thousand pictures of me, but I won't mind. She hasn't been able to do things like that ever so why not.

"Mya, can I come in?" Dad said.

"Yeah, sure," I answered.

"Your mother told me the news about this homecoming dance. I thought that was only for high schoolers!" Dad said.

"Usually it's that way, but Springville does more of a junior homecoming dance. I don't think it will be exactly like a high school dance, but what do I know? I'm new to all this. Right, dad." I said sarcastically.

"Well, it doesn't seem like you're new to all of this. You are moving along pretty swiftly at your new school. You have friends, you started a school club, and now you're going to a dance. Wow. And what's this I hear about a date? I thought Steven was just a friend!" Dad asked in his stern voice.

"He is just a friend. Just two friends going together. I knew mom would exaggerate. It's not even like that. Were just friend's dad." I assured my dad.

"That's what everyone says. I'll be keeping a close eye on him. But what I really want to discuss is, you not going." Dad said.
"
What! I'm going dad. Why would you say that?" I said.

"I just do not think that it's a good idea. Those girls will most likely be there, and I don't want another bullying episode to occur. We need to get down to the bottom of all of the troubles that you've been having and contact these girl's parents. Who knows what they might try to pull at this dance Mya. Seriously." Dad said.

"But dad. I'll be with Steven! He's a good friend. He will have my back, and besides there will be plenty of teachers there. I will make sure to stay with people. I won't wander off anywhere." I cried.

"I know this means a lot to you, but as a father, this really concerns me," Dad said.

"Dad, I'll be fine. Don't worry. My guidance counselor should be there and he is always looking out for me. Mr. Davids cares about me! Please, don't worry." I said.

"Alright Mya, but just know that I will be contacting the school and asking them to keep a close eye on you at this dance. As well as dropping you off and waiting outside for you." Dad said.

"Okay, dad," I said, and looked away from my dad.

I cannot believe my dad overreacted like that. I mean, I get it. He's a dad. Dads are supposed to be protective of their daughters, especially when they're crippled. When he was talking to me about not going, I just wanted to blurt out and tell him that I'm magical. If dad knew that I had a magical power, he wouldn't worry as much. I can protect myself now, and those bullies know it. They didn't try to touch me this last time. They only hurt me with their words.

Now, I need to find a dress. I think I want to just wear a black dress. I'm not really into too many colors. A nice black dress, with my dreads into a bun. Steven could match, or not. Totally up to him, but I know that my mom will be harassing us for pictures.

There is so much on my mind, so much to do, and now my magical power to learn. Not only learn, but keep a secret. It shouldn't be too hard though. I don't plan on randomly moving things with my mind. For now, at least. I wonder if this is my only magical power. Who knows. I could have other powers that I have yet to discover.

One cool thing about this power is, I don't have to get up to get the remote control anymore. I'm able to just move it with my mind now, and it'll come to me. Learning my power has its benefits.

It is true, that everything is becoming overwhelming. But it's giving me more purpose and confidence. Being busy isn't always a bad thing. Yes, it makes me tired but so what. Who cares about being tired. I spent years being homeschooled, and laying around the house with absolutely nothing else going on for myself. Those days made me feel so unpretty. Now, I'm not feeling totally pretty or completely confident. But I'm making progress.

Getting through this dance will big a major step for me. I hope everything goes well. Dad is right about those bullies. They will most likely be there. It's a shame that they're even allowed to go. After all that they have done. That could be my fault too, I haven't really reported them to the principal. I don't know their names. I just try my best to get away from them. Plus, I didn't want to make them any angrier than they were. Things could get worse for me if they got suspended.

All I can do is stay away from them and hope for the best. But I won't miss all the fun school activities just because of those bullies. If that was the case then there would be no need to continue going to Springville. This time if they mess with me, they will have something coming for them. I mean it.

On a lighter note, now it's time to get my mom ready for some shopping. Who am I really kidding? She's probably readier than I am. She's probably waiting by the front door or already looking at dresses online for me. This should be fun.

When I find something, I'll tell Steven. Actually, I'll send him pictures to his phone of my outfit. I'm sure he would probably want to match, even though we are just friends.

I hope he's just as excited for this as I am. Probably not. He wasn't even going to go in the first place. I guess because he doesn't have many friends so he would be alone just looking around. If Steven were going, I probably wouldn't go either. Corrine never responded to our texts. So, I'm guessing she doesn't want to be bothered with the dance. She's pretty quiet so it actually may make her extremely uncomfortable. Who knows. She could've at least responded. Maybe she will tomorrow, but tonight is all about dress shopping with mom. Yes, I have to go now. I don't want to wait because I'm anxious and so is mom.

My mom and I leave to go shopping at the mall for a dress. Dad stays behind and tells them to get something appropriate for a thirteen-year-old. My mom and I chuckle and laugh at dad before walking out of the door.

Chapter 10

The magic doesn't stop the party, it saves the party

It is Friday and I'm super excited for tonight. I could hardly pay attention in any of my classes today. I tried to get home as fast as possible, just so I could prepare myself. I will start with washing my dreads and making them look nice. Mom has taught me all different styles for dreads, but I think I'll go with a high bun on top of my head.

The dance starts at seven tonight, and I'm already so nervous. I have a few hours before the dance starts and butterflies are tickling my stomach. Mom said this is normal though. I've never felt this nervous. I didn't even feel this nervous when those girls were following me down the hall. For a split second, I considered not going. Only a split second. No time for backing out now. My dress is so nice. Mom picked it out and everything. She has way better taste than me. This dress is way better than all of the dresses that I picked out. The ones I picked out were so boring and old looking.

I just have a gut feeling that something is going to go wrong. I'm not sure what, but something. Like maybe Steven will cancel because he never really wanted to go in the first place, or my dress will get ruined, or maybe even the dance will get canceled for some strange reason. I could just be stressing myself out for no reason. I don't know, but I need to just breathe.

My phone started to vibrate loudly from across the room. I didn't feel like getting it, but I needed to see who was texting me. It could be Steven texting me about the dance. I used my power to move the phone closer to me. I squinted my eyes really tight while staring at the phone and bringing it to me.

I looked at my phone and there were text messages from Steven and Corrine, which appeared to be a semi-argument or dispute between them.

"So, you guys decided to go to the homecoming dance without me? Some friend's you guys are." Corrine said in the group chat.

"Ummm, last I checked you never even responded to the group chat! You completely ignored the entire conversation, so don't try to pull that crap." Steven said.

"Did either of you think to even ask me why? No, you didn't. I guess you didn't care." Corrine said.

"Oh, please Corrine. Please. It's not a big deal. I have other things to be worrying about here at home." Steven said.

"Whatever," Corrine replied.

Finally, I interjected into the conversation after it ended over thirty minutes ago.

"Corrine, do you want to go? I heard that they are selling tickets at the door since there were tickets left." I said.

"Yeah, you should come. Don't be a big baby." Steven said.

"Corrine? You coming?" I asked.

"Aren't you guys going as dates or whatever?" Corrine asked.

"Girl, are you coming or not? Make up your mind. We would all be together." I said.

"If I decide to go, I'll see you guys there," Corrine said.

"I guess," I replied.

That was the end of that conversation, and I couldn't believe that she was actually mad. She was the one who never even responded to us when I first asked about the homecoming dance. That was so weird. Corrine is my friend, but whatever. I can't get all rattled up over that conversation. I need to be getting ready for tonight.

"Mom!" I yelled downstairs for her to come help me.

"What!" I responded back.

"Aren't you going to help me?" I said.

"Now? It's early." Mom replied.

"Not really, come on mom. Before you know it, it'll be time to leave for the dance. I don't want to rush and everything has to be perfect." I said.

"In a minute Mya, In a minute." Mom said.

This dance is a serious deal. It may be pretty corny or lame to others, but not to me. I may end up being really bored at this dance, but at least I can say that I went.

Mom asked me if I wanted to wear make-up to the dance, ugh I don't really know about that right now. I thought about it, but I may end up looking like a clown and that's no fun. I'm already a joke at Springville. I know It will be a complete shock to even see me there. I don't need anything else making me stand out. I already stand out, but the make-up would make it worse.

Eye shadow is definitely going to be a no, but maybe some eye liner with mascara.
God knows I won't be wearing any lipstick!
Mom says that I'm not old enough for that anyway. No problem here.

I wonder how Steven is going to feel walking into the dance with me as I use my walker. I hope that it won't embarrass him. Maybe I won't use it. It's been a while since I walked without using it, but why not try. I'll just have to see. Right now, I'm feeling confident about it. I know for a fact mom and dad won't agree nor allow it. So hopefully Steven won't care. I'm sure people won't be looking for us. They probably won't even notice that we are there since the lights will be off. I think I want to be fashionably late to avoid people seeing me when I first walk in.

I have my outfit out on my bed, and I feel like something is missing. I have my dress and shoes but that's it. I wish I had some glitter, jewelry or something to add. Oh, my goodness. Who am I turning into? I never wore any of that stuff before, or even cared too. I guess I just want to fit in tonight and not look crazy. Steven said he will be wearing black to match me. I'm sure he'll look nice. I told him to leave the overalls at home Ha-ha.

My dad just peaked into my room to be nosey. He probably wanted to know if I started to get dressed yet. Mom and I didn't let him see the dress when we came home from the mall. Mom told him that he couldn't see the dress until I was completely dressed and ready to head out the door.

Dad wasn't too happy about that but he trusts mom's judgment. My dress is perfect for a thirteen-year-old to wear at this kind of thing. It's the perfect homecoming dress for me. I still can't believe I didn't know about this dance. I really thought only the high school did homecomings. Well, I was wrong and I'm glad Steven and I agreed to go together.

I know mom and dad are going to definitely assume that we have a crush on each other or something now, but that would be false. We are strictly friends going to a dance together. We are cool people, as dad would say. I wish my grandmother could be here. She would probably say, I told you so. She always told me I was super special. Boy was she dropping hints to me. I hope that she is watching down on me. If she were here, I would tell her about my magical power. Grandma was always really good at keeping secrets. We would share secrets all the time, and she never told mom or dad. My grandma was so cool. She would also be helping me with school, the bullying and everything else. She would love Steven and Corrine. Really miss her, especially now that I actually have a lot of things going on. She only got to see me when cerebral palsy was my entire life.

Thinking about my grandma makes me even more excited for tonight. She loved to listen to music and dance. She would be very disappointed If I let those bullies keep me from going to the dance. She was a tough old lady with backbone. Now that I think about it, she probably had magical powers and knew I'd get them one day. I wonder if mom knows, but just never said anything to me. What if mom has a power but has kept it a secret. In all the magical movies that I've watched, magic was in the bloodline. I know movies are fake, but hey. It could be true. If mom has a superpower I will find out, sooner or later. I'll find out secretly or just come out and ask her. I can't be the only one in my family with a power. Technically, dad could have them but he would've told us. Dad is too blunt and is bad at keeping secrets. The whole family knows that. Dad kinda has a big mouth. So, I know he doesn't have any magical power. I'm really thinking that mom does. Or maybe grandma did, and it skipped mom. I don't know. I just don't want to be alone in this.

I think I will tell my mom about my power soon though, but for now, I need for her to bring her butt upstairs to do my dreads. My mom knows how to do my dreads nicely. Better than me. When I decided to get them, mom did her research online and found so many cute styles for me to wear. She's really the greatest.

"Mom!" I yelled at the top of my lungs.

"Oh God Mya, I'm coming. You have time!" Mom said.

"Well, I want to be ready before Steven gets here," I said.

"Alright Mya, Alright. I'm coming." Mom yelled.

I'm surprised that mom isn't the one rushing me! Well maybe I am getting dressed a little too early, but the excitement won't leave me alone. Also, my mom must be forgetting that It takes me a little longer to get dressed because of my condition. So, I really need to get started.

Mom finally comes up the stairs to my room and opens the door. She looks at me and smiles.

"Girl I'm here…" Mom said.

"I need you to do my hair mom. I want the high bun with a few pieces left out like you did when we went out with dad's family." I said.

"Shouldn't you put your clothes on first Mya?" I think so. You wouldn't want to mess your hair up." Mom said.

Mom is right, I probably should get dressed first. I hopped in the shower, and when I got out of the shower mom came back up to help me get ready. Time is actually winding up. I told mom that would happen. I won't have to rush, but Steven will be here in less than an hour.

Mom helped me with my dress and hair then she called dad in to see what I looked like. This should be interesting. Dad hasn't seen me in a dress in such a long time.

"You look stunning baby girl," Dad said while staring at me. I think he's trying to decide if the dress is appropriate enough. Dad is crazy.

"Thank you, daddy. Mom picked the dress out. She has great taste! She also did my hair." I said, reminding him that mom was the one who picked the dress out so he couldn't say anything.

The dress isn't revealing but it is strapless, so my shoulders are showing. I know deep down inside dad doesn't like it. Oh well.
"You like her dress and hair honey?" Mom asked dad.

"Eh, not too happy about the dress being strapless. But she looks nice. What shoes are you going to wear?" Dad said.

"These black flats." I showed dad the flats.

I kinda wish that I could wear heels, but then again, I wouldn't. Who am I kidding? That's totally not me, and besides, I wouldn't be able to even walk in them. I'd fall flat on my face.

"What time is Steven supposed to get here?" Dad asked.

"Pretty soon right Mya?" Mom asked.

"Yes, He should be here any minute now actually so I'm going to head downstairs to wait for him," I said in a nervous tone.

The butterflies are having another party in my stomach. I am beyond nervous and excited all at the same time. I just want him to be here already so that we can just get the initial walking in part over with. Once I get there, the butterflies should leave my stomach. I hope. I'm also starving so hopefully they have some pretty good refreshments there.

Suddenly I hear the doorbell ring, my heart started to race as I went downstairs with my parents. Steven is on time and ready to go. He looks amazing. The boy cleans up really nice. He said on a black sweater, with black pants. He also has on a gold bracelet. I knew I should've had some jewelry or something.

"Whoa Mya, you look great," Steven said.

"Thanks, not too bad yourself," I said.

"One more thing to top this off, Mya," Mom said.

"What! What!" I said with excitement.

"Here you go love." Mom said while showing me a gold necklace with a heart charm.

"Wow mom, this is awesome. Thank you. Can you put it on me?" I said with joy.

"Yes, of course. I thought tonight would be perfect for it." Mom said.

"That's really cool Mrs. Iverson. That's cool." Steven said.

"Well, thank you Mr. Sharp." Mom said.

"Mya, your grandmother bought me a necklace just like this when I was around your age for my homecoming dance. Thought I'd make it a tradition." Mom said.

"I'm glad you did mom. Now I'm really ready to go." I said.

"Dad, Stevens mom will take us! You really don't have to! You can pick me up though." I said while winking and making faces at my mom trying to get her attention. Mom will tell dad to let me just go with Steven.

"Mr. Iverson, you can drive us if you'd like, but Mya is right. My mom can drive also." Steven added.

"Well, alright. You can go with Steven and his mom. But I will be there to pick you up. You hear me?" Dad asked, as if I wasn't standing right in front of him.

"Yes! I hear you. Now goodbye mom and dad. Love you guys." I said and kinda rush out of the door with Steven.

"Goodbye Mr. and Mrs. Iverson," Steven said as we left out of my house.

We get into his mom's truck, and I immediately get upset about having to climb up into the truck because Steven is going to have to help me. As awkward as that is going to be.

"Do you need help, Mya?" Steven asked.

"Definitely, I'll end up falling and totally messing up my hair." I replied, as we both started to laugh.

"Be careful with her!" Stevens mom yelled to the back of the truck as she watched us struggle.

We finally get into the truck, and his mom pulls off.

"Hello!" I said.

"Hi, Ms. Mya. I hear about you every day. I'm glad that my boy has a friend." Stevens mom replied.

So, we arrive at the school, and Steven helps me out of the car. He also grabs my hand before we walk into the building. He's a sure gentleman just trying to make sure that I'm not freaking out.
"
Have a great time! Drink lots of punch, and eat the cookies!" Stevens mom said.

"We will!" Both of us said at the same time. We are at the door and still haven't gone in yet. Steven says, "Let's go!" When he says that my heart drops into my stomach, but I'm going to just go ahead. Can't chicken out now, my ride left. Ha-ha.

We enter the school, and Steven hands the guy at the cafeteria door our dance tickets. After that, we went inside. Finally, we were inside of the dance. It was really dark and super loud. The music was extremely loud that I couldn't even hear myself think. Steven had to yell at me, to get my attention. But I guess this is a good thing because nobody is really looking at us or paying us any attention at all. This is a good thing.

Steven and I head over to the refreshments table. There's punch, cookies, cake, and sandwiches. Steven started to eat, but I wasn't hungry. I tend to be clumsy and didn't want to mess up my dress. But this is cool so far. This dance is pretty much what I assumed it would be.

All of a sudden somebody tapped me on my shoulder, and It was Corrine. Corrine decided to come! And she looks amazing. I thought she was a pretty girl before, but whoa. This was another side of her. I guess we all clean up pretty nice.

"Well, Well, Well, The three amigos together at the dance. So, happy that you decided to show up miss attitude." Steven said, as we all laughed and hugged.

Chapter 11

A Magical Night To Remember For The Unpretty

The dance is still going well, and I am so happy that Corrine decided to come. Now it is the three of us, just eating refreshments and enjoying the music. Corrine actually looks like she wants to dance. I hope that i'm not holding them back from going out to the dance floor and completely having a good time.

"You guys should go out there and dance. Don't let me stand in your way. Trust me, watching you guys dance will be enough enjoyment from the side. I can't even imagine how you guys dance." I said while laughing.

"Nah, I'm good for now, unless you wanna go dance, Corrine?" Steven asked.

"Uhm, I'm good for now also. You guys look so nice." Corrine said.

"Thanks, girl," I replied.
"Thank ya. You look great." Steven replied.

"Mya, you can dance later too if you want. We'll help you. You can leave your walker off to the side, and we will help you dance with us." Steven said.

"Yes, Mya. Steven is right. Do you want to dance?" Corrine asked.

"Umm, I don't know about that guys. That's a very nice gesture, but I'll probably have to pass on that. Dancing really isn't my thing. I don't even think I've ever danced in front of people. Only my mom and dad," I said.

"Come on Mya, think about it. The dance will be over before you know it and later you might regret not dancing for even a minute," Corrine added.

"Still, don't think I'm going out there. But you guys are great. I'm so glad that I have you both," I said.

I am looking around the dance to see if any of those bullies are here, and I spotted the girl that I used my magic on. She doesn't see me, but I see her. I sure hope it stays that way. I don't want any drama or craziness tonight. Just pure fun. I want to give mom and dad a good report when they pick me up. Especially dad since he was really worried about me coming in the first place.

Steven is eating everything at the refreshment table, while Corrine and I just kinda stand to the side and watch everyone dance. I even see Mr. Davids dancing. He's so cool. Actually, he's the absolute coolest. There's actually a few teachers dancing a little bit. Springville is a cool school for the most part. Mr. Davids said that every school has bullies, although some more than others. So, I won't hold that against Springville. But, Springville could do a better job at punishing bullies because they never get in trouble. She shouldn't even be allowed here. Yet, she is here having a great time.

I just hope and pray that she doesn't see me or any of her little friends that follow her every move. I don't really remember what any of her friends look like because I tried to look straight ahead and not look at them. All I can do is pray and hope that even if they do see me, they will be smart enough to leave me alone. Especially in front of all of these teachers. They would definitely get in trouble. It's a shame that this is on my mind when I should be focusing on having a good time with my friends. I just need to breathe and relax. Whatever is going to happen will happen.

The DJ has been playing pretty good music so far. There has been a mixture of music played tonight. They've played Beyoncé, Katy Perry, Bruno Mars, and a bunch of other music artist that people my age love. Every time they played a song that I liked, there was a strong urge to dance. I must be honest. I'm not quite sure where it came from, but it came. Maybe I'm happy. Maybe I'm finally comfortable or feeling confident. I'm liking this. I see a few girls who came to my first meeting for The Unpretty Project and donated to our clothing drive. Some waved, and some gave me a hug. After this dance, I really want to do more with The Unpretty Project. So much is happening and I'm so excited.

"Hey Mya, Corrine and I really want you to dance. Come on, please. Just for a second," Steven pleaded.

"Yeah, come on. We won't go to the center of the dance floor. We'll stay off to the side. Let's do it, girl." Corrine anxiously said. She appears to have ants in her pants. I knew she really wanted to dance. I could tell.

I really don't want to dance. I know this will end badly, but I'm going to give it a try. I should close my eyes and dance.

"Come on Mya. Don't be shy," Corrine said.

I think this is the most excited that I've ever seen Corrine. She looks so happy, I just couldn't say no. I left my walker over by the refreshment table. Steven and Corrine said they will help me keep an eye on it. They both grab my arms and go to the dance floor. We are dancing to a song called uptown funk. I really like this song. It always comes on the radio when I'm in the car with my mom. This isn't as bad as I thought it would be. The three of us are dancing together, and I don't even care if I look silly. I'm having fun. Steven and Corrine are true friends for holding my hands to help me dance along with them. They could have just left me alone. I wouldn't mind, but this really shows me how much they care. Finally, I have real friends. This is a really good feeling. Nothing could kill my vibe at this point.

I glance over at the refreshment table and my walker is missing. Steven and Corrine don't see it either so it's not just me.

"Don't worry Mya, we will find your walker," Steven said.

"I knew something like this would happen, I bet you it's those bullies. They spotted me here and are trying to mess with me once again." I yelled!

"You were just having a ball, don't let them change that. We will find it. One of our teachers could've moved it away from the refreshment table too. Let's not jump to conclusions." Corrine added.

"I'm sure of it Corrine," I said.

"I want to speak with Mr. David to ask him to keep an eye out. Can you guys help me walk over to him?" I asked.

"Of course," Steven said.

When we got to Mr. Davids he was very happy to see me but could tell that something was bothering me. I asked him if he had seen my walker, but he didn't. He informed all the teachers, and everyone said they'd look. Steven and Corrine left me over by Mr. Davids while they looked around. Suddenly, I glance back over to the refreshment table and it was there. Back like it never left. I told Mr. Davids and texted my friends. Steven and Corrine helped me get back to my walker.

When I got back to my walker, I decided to go to the bathroom. Steven and Corrine asked if I needed their help. I told them no. I had a plan. Finally, I'm going to teach these bullies a valuable lesson. They will never forget the magical homecoming dance. I just know that they will follow me, they won't be able to help it. They will look for me and assume that I went to the bathroom. The only reason why my walker was returned is because teachers started to look for it and they got scared. I just can't believe nobody saw them with it. I'm sick of them being bullies and getting away with it.

I am in the bathroom waiting and so far, nobody has come in. I've been in the bathroom for over five minutes. I'll wait another five or six minutes. If I wait too long Steven and Corrine will come looking for me. I don't want that to happen. These bullies need one on one time with me and my new power. The first time obviously didn't scare them. But this time I know how to properly use my power. So, they can mess with the crippled dread headed girl if they want to. I'm waiting.

I keep receiving text messages from Steven and Corrine. I told them I was coming back now. I guess I should leave and go back to the dance. I was just so totally fed up with these people messing with me. Mom texted me too and asked how it was going. I told her it was going great. I'm not going to worry mom and dad about my walker going missing. They will drive up here so quick and nobody needs that. That would ruin my night. Mom would be so stressed and crying. Yeah, I'll pass. They don't need to know every little thing that happens. I'm growing up. Somethings I need to handle myself.

As I leave the bathroom, to my surprise there they were. They didn't come into the bathroom, but they waited for me to leave. Sounds very familiar. I should've known. Here we were, standing in the very same spot that we were standing in when they threw me to the ground. Along with my walker, almost breaking it. But this time I am ready. I am confident.

We stared at each other for a minute until finally, a guy said, "so, I guess you think that you're pretty cool now huh? Well, you're not."

"Thank you for your opinion. I guess you think I'm pretty cool though huh? Since you stalk me. You follow me around like I am some sort of a celebrity. Thanks for the confidence boost." I replied with a smirk on my face.

"You have a smart mouth for a girl who just got here, and you're a cripple." He said.

"Oh, don't forget she's some sort of witch or freak." Someone else in their little group said.

"You're right. I am a witch. Would you like me to cast a spell on you? Let me go get my wand." I replied cracking up in their faces.

"Pretty funny. You know if you weren't so crippled, we'd let you join our friend group. But nah, you'd cramp our style." The girl said who pushed me to the ground.

"I have friends. I wouldn't be friends with people like you if you paid me." I replied.

All of a sudden, I heard sounds of loud feet coming at me. It was Steven and Corrine.

"Mya, are you okay? Are they bothering you?" Steven asked.

"They're being jerks as usual. But I'm not bothered." I replied.

Steven and Corrine stood beside me as those jerks started to laugh loudly. I'm wondering why teachers are never around when they start this up. They should be walking the halls to make sure everyone is safe. My group will be addressing this issue to the principal on Monday.

"Oh, there's more freaks." The bullies started to chant.

As we started to walk away, the bullies pushed Steven and Corrine to the ground first. As they charged towards me, I felt the magic in my body rising up and I had a decision to make. If I used my powers, exposure would definitely happen. But at this point, I don't care. They were given to me for a reason.

I raised my hand up so they would stop coming towards us, and stood strong. As I stood strong, I stared at them and used my power to throw them all around the hall. It was hilarious. They were flying all over the place, even banging against the walls. When I stopped, they just laid there in silence. Steven and Corrine stared at me and I told them to come on.

"Let's get out of here, I'll explain at the dance," I said.

Steven and Corrine looked so confused and afraid. They probably thought that they were dreaming. I was exposed. Well, not to the whole world. Maybe they will keep my secret. I don't think the bullies will tell people. They would sound absolutely insane. Who would believe them? I wouldn't. Magic isn't supposed to be real, but it is.

When we got back to the dance, Steven and Corrine just stopped and stared at me again like I was an alien or something.

"What the heck was that?" Steven asked.

"Yeah, like should I be scared?" Corrine asked.

"I've been meaning to tell you guys but this is really new to me as well. After the last time they bullied me, I got angry and discovered that I was magical. When I got angry, I used my powers on those kids without even trying. Then I went home and did some research. It's real guys. Magic is real. And I have it.

"Well, we see that!" Steven said.

"So, what now? What are these powers for?" Corrine asked.

"I don't know actually. Maybe protection against mean people. Maybe God thought that I needed some other strength because of my condition. Without this power, those bullies would've really hurt me. I wouldn't be able to fight back. So, I'm actually grateful for it, but please do not tell anyone. My parents don't even know. This must stay a secret." I said.

"Well sure, but what about those bullies? They may tell the whole school!" Corrine said.

"Yeah, then the secrets out," Steven added.

"I don't think they will. Can you imagine them going around telling people that I have superpowers? They would sound insane and people would think that they're lying, or crazy at the least. Nobody believes that magic is real until they experience it for themselves. I didn't believe in it before." I said.

"Well, I guess you're right. Your secret is safe with me." Steven said.

"It is safe with me too. Just don't use them on me." Corrine said laughing.

"This is actually extremely cool Mya," Steven said.

"Thank you, guys, now can we go back to partying? The dance is almost over."

"Heck yes!" Steven and Corrine both replied.

So, we danced for a little bit, and I noticed that those bullies never came back into the dance. I literally scared the pants off of them. They probably called their mommy's and daddies to pick them up. Good for them. They deserved to feel scared for once. The shoe was finally on the other foot.

The music stopped and all I heard was a familiar voice get on the microphone and it was Mr. Davids. He was thanking everyone for coming out and having a good time. He mentioned a spring dance since this one was so successful. That should be fun! Another dance for my friends and I to come to. Next time it'll bully free. I think that they learned their lesson. As Mr. Davids concludes his speech he says something that totally caught my attention.

"Before we end the night, I would like to call up a very brave soul who has inspired me and many others here at Springville. She has not been here for even a full semester yet, but has made such an impact. Mya Iverson would you please say a few words to your fellow students."

My first thoughts were, "how dare he embarrass me like this, heck no I'm not going up there." But my second thoughts were, "Mr. Davids is so nice, and if he thinks I should say something then why not."

Steven helped me walk up to the microphone, and I look to the back of the cafeteria and see my parents watching. Mr. Davids must've had this planned all along and invited my parents. Wow. Sneaky people all around me. Well, I guess I should say something, and not just stand here looking crazy. Here goes nothing.

Mya's Homecoming speech:

Hello, everyone.

My fellow Springville students. I'm not really a speaker, but I'm grateful that Mr. Davids thought enough of me to invite me up here. Today's dance has been really fun and I hope that you all will come out to the spring dance as well.

Some of you are staring at me, wondering who the heck I am. But that is because you choose not to see me. I've been coming to school every day, trying my best to fit in. I know some of you are wondering why I use a walker, or why my speech isn't the best. But it is because I have cerebral palsy. I hope you all have heard of it at some point in your lives. It has been my whole life, until now.

Please don't judge me based on my condition. I'm a kid just like you. I'm a thirteen-year-old just like you. I even started a school club here called, The Unpretty Project. There are flyers everywhere. Some of you donated to the clothing drive that I had here at Springville, but many of you didn't. I hope that after today we could all go to school in perfect harmony. We should be able to be friends no matter what someone looks like or what disability they may have.

My experience here at Springville has been exhausting and tough. It has also been hard dealing with the bullying here at Springville. But I wouldn't let that stop me from coming to school. I've waited so long to be a student and make friends. Nothing was getting in my way. I hope that after today, when you see me, you won't just see my condition. But you will see a regular kid just trying to experience a normal childhood. Thanks, Mr. Davids, and goodnight everyone.

That wasn't easy, but it was worth it. My time here at Springville has been interesting. Some good, and some bad. I can't wait to see what the future has in store. I'm pretty darn proud of myself. Apparently so are Mom, Dad, and Mr. Davids. All three of them are crying. Typical. Ha-ha.

After the dance, I said goodbye to my friends and went home with my very proud parents. Tonight, I will sleep like a baby, with no worries. I will also say a prayer, thanking God and grandma for my magical power. It gave me super strength.

I will go to school next week with confidence. The eighth grade will be a breeze, and high school is not ready for me.

What a magical night...

Ten Things to do when you feel Unpretty!

- Find out what you're good at, everyone's good at something
- Say nice things to yourself in the mirror
- Be around people who love you
- Do things that make you happy
- Laugh a lot
- Remind yourself, that you're not alone
- Write down all the things you like about yourself
- Join clubs, groups and positive organizations
- Develop your own personal style
- Have quiet time with yourself and breathe

The Author

Miranda A. Reid was born in New Jersey, where she also grew up on April 4th, 1995. Miranda is a young woman who desires to make an impact on the lives of young children and young adults. She graduated from Rowan University where she received her bachelor's degree in sociology. She is also the Founder and President of a Nonprofit community service mentoring program called, The Unpretty Project. She loves to give back to her community and be a leader for young women. She plans to continue her education, and her career in writing. She has always written short stories and poetry since she was a young child, dreaming to one day publish her own book. She has experience working with young children, young adults, and children with extreme disadvantages and disabilities. She is a rising author, mentor, leader and youth advocate.

Your disability does not define you. We all have super strengths. Everyday write down something that you are good at, and something that makes you special. Use the blank pages below.

I hope that with this, you will find that you are magical.

So You Think You're Unpretty?

With A Little Magic.

So You Think You're Unpretty?

With A Little Magic.

So You Think You're Unpretty?

With A Little Magic.

So You Think You're Unpretty?

With A Little Magic.

So You Think You're Unpretty?

With A Little Magic.

Made in the USA
Las Vegas, NV
17 June 2021

24859566R00132